*Powerful, prominent, proud—the Oklahoma Wentworths'
greatest fortune was family. So when they discovered that
pregnant mom-to-be Sabrina Jensen was carrying the
newest Wentworth heir—and had vanished without a
trace—they vowed to...Follow That Baby!*

Rachel Jensen: The wild twin with
a penchant for scrapes, she'd always
found gentle words and comforting
hugs from Sabrina. But now her
straight-and-narrow sister was
alone—and expecting—so
Rachel transformed herself into the
take-charge twin whose only
weakness was...

Riley Hunter: This small-town sheriff craved more
than desk duty drudgery, so the prospect of a mom-
to-be on the hoof was particularly enticing. But
when he met the alleged runaway face-to-face, he
discovered he was in way over his head....

Sabrina Jensen: With precious little time before
her baby's birth, Sabrina was still keeping mum
about her mystery nest and keeping fit with Lamaze
classes, where a fellow first-timer felt moved to
alert the mighty Wentworths....

* * * *

Don't miss
THE MILLIONAIRE AND THE PREGNANT PAUPER
by Christie Ridgway, next month's Follow That Baby
title, available in Yours Truly.

Dear Reader,

All of us at Silhouette Desire send you our best wishes for a joyful holiday season. December brings six original, deeply touching love stories warm enough to melt your heart!

This month, bestselling author Cait London continues her beloved miniseries THE TALLCHIEFS with the story of MAN OF THE MONTH Nick Palladin in *The Perfect Fit*. This corporate cowboy's attempt to escape his family's matchmaking has him escorting a *Tallchief* down the aisle. Silhouette Desire welcomes the cross-line continuity FOLLOW THAT BABY to the line with Elizabeth Bevarly's *The Sheriff and the Impostor Bride*. And those irresistible bad-boy James brothers return in Cindy Gerard's *Marriage, Outlaw Style*, part of the OUTLAW HEARTS miniseries. When a headstrong bachelor and his brassy-but-beautiful childhood rival get stranded, they wind up in a 6lb., 12oz. bundle of trouble!

Talented author Susan Crosby's third book in THE LONE WOLVES miniseries, *His Ultimate Temptation*, will entrance you with this hero's primitive, unyielding desire to protect his once-wife and their willful daughter. A rich playboy sweeps a sensible heroine from her humdrum life in Shawna Delacorte's Cinderella story, *The Millionaire's Christmas Wish*. And Eileen Wilks weaves an emotional, edge-of-your-seat drama about a fierce cop and the delicate lady who poses as his newlywed bride in *Just a Little Bit Married?*

These poignant, sensuous books fill any Christmas stocking—and every reader's heart with the glow of holiday romance. Enjoy!

Best regards,
Joan Marlow Golan
Senior Editor

Please address questions and book requests to:
Silhouette Reader Service
U.S.: 3010 Walden Ave., P.O. Box 1325, Buffalo, NY 14269
Canadian: P.O. Box 609, Fort Erie, Ont. L2A 5X3

Elizabeth Bevarly

THE SHERIFF AND THE IMPOSTOR BRIDE

SILHOUETTE *Desire*

Published by Silhouette Books

America's Publisher of Contemporary Romance

Special thanks and acknowledgment are given to Elizabeth Bevarly for her contribution to the *Follow That Baby* series.

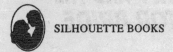 SILHOUETTE BOOKS

ISBN 0-373-76184-8

THE SHERIFF AND THE IMPOSTOR BRIDE

Copyright © 1998 by Harlequin Books S.A.

Printed in U.S.A.

Books by Elizabeth Bevarly

Silhouette Desire

An Unsuitable Man for the Job #724
Jake's Christmas #753
A Lawless Man #856
*A Dad like Daniel #908
*The Perfect Father #920
*Dr. Daddy #933
†*Father of the Brat* #993
†*Father of the Brood* #1005
†*Father on the Brink* #1016
‡*Roxy and the Rich Man* #1053
‡*Lucy and the Loner* #1063
‡*Georgia Meets Her Groom* #1083
**Bride of the Bad Boy #1124
**Beauty and the Brain #1130
**The Virgin and the Vagabond #1136
The Sheriff and the Impostor Bride #1184

Silhouette Special Edition

Destinations South #557
Close Range #590
Donovan's Chance #639
Moriah's Mutiny #676
Up Close #737
Hired Hand #803
Return Engagement #844

*From Here to Maternity
†From Here to Paternity
‡The Family McCormick
**Blame It on Bob

ELIZABETH BEVARLY

is an honors graduate of the University of Louisville and achieved her dream of writing full-time before she even turned thirty! At heart, she is also an avid voyager who once helped navigate a friend's thirty-five-foot sailboat across the Bermuda Triangle. "I really love to travel," says this self-avowed beach bum. "To me, it's the best education a person can give to herself." Her dream is to one day have her own sailboat, a beautifully renovated older model forty-two-footer, and to enjoy the freedom and tranquillity seafaring can bring. Elizabeth likes to think she has a lot in common with the characters she creates—people who know love and life go hand in hand. And she's getting some firsthand experience with motherhood, as well—she and her husband have a four-year-old son, Eli.

For Mom and Aunt Dot—
my favorite set of twins.

One

Lost in thought as he scribbled down his latest report on the notorious howling Barker family, Sheriff Riley Hunter jerked open the bottom right-hand drawer of his desk, felt around blindly, then frowned when his fingers encountered nothing but a stack of Louis L'Amour paperbacks. He pushed his chair away from the desk, shoved his ink black, razor-straight, shoulder-length hair out of his eyes, and gazed down at the drawer. The big empty space beside the battered novels, exactly the size of a box of Lorna Doone cookies, attested to the severity of the crime.

Theft, plain and simple, had come to Wallace Canyon, Oklahoma. What was the world coming to?

Who the hell had run off with his stash of Lorna Doones? Riley wondered, his anger compounding. Virgil, doubtless, he decided. His deputy sheriff had an even bigger sweet tooth than Riley had, and regardless of the fact that Virgil Bybee was sworn to uphold the law, he'd probably figured that a crime like Lorna Doone pilfering would go unnoticed in a dinky little community like Wallace Canyon.

And who had named it Wallace Canyon anyway? Riley won-

dered further, not for the first time since his self-inflicted reloca-
tion here six months earlier. There were no canyons in the
Oklahoma panhandle. Wallace Flat would have been much more
appropriate. Still, he'd learned almost right away that in Wallace
Canyon, not a whole lot made sense. Mainly because not a whole
lot happened.

"Virgil!" he called out as he unfolded his slim, six-foot frame
from behind his desk. "Where the hell are my Lorna Doones?"

Riley cocked his head to listen for any incriminating sounds of
cookie crunching or falling crumbs, but the only thing he heard
was the faint crackle of Rosario's radio down the hall, tuned to
the only country-western station—hell, the only radio station, period—within earshot of the tiny town. The soft, easy crooning of
a female voice soothed him some. Patsy Cline, he realized with
a fond smile when he listened harder. Wasn't *nobody* singing
today who could touch that woman. No, sir.

"Virgil!" he tried again, pushing the thought away.

The slow scuff of boots along the linoleum outside Riley's
office eventually found its way down the hall. Then Virgil Bybee's head appeared in Riley's doorway, halfway down, as if the
younger man were bent at the waist and unwilling to reveal anything below the neck.

Incriminating behavior if ever there was such a thing, Riley
decided, his instincts, as always, unimpeachable. He hadn't sur-
vived almost ten years on the Tulsa PD because of his good luck
and good looks alone, after all.

"You bellowed?" Virgil asked mildly.

"Where the hell are my Lorna Doones?" Riley demanded
again without preamble.

"Shoot, Riley, how should I know?" But anxiously, Virgil
swiped his fingers across his upper lip.

Riley reared his head back, settled one hand on a trim hip, the
other on the butt of his pistol, and noticed that Virgil duly noted
the stance. For one long moment, he said nothing. Then he stated
with all the menace he could muster, "Virgil, I want those cookies
apprehended and returned to my jurisdiction—namely this here
drawer—" he pointed down at the cookies' usual resting place
"—no later than three o'clock this afternoon. You got that?"

Virgil nodded silently, his shaggy blond hair falling over his forehead with the gesture, his blue eyes widening at the warning. Then, before Riley had a chance to comment further, the deputy flung his arm out, rattling the piece of flimsy paper attached to his hand. "This came in over the fax a few minutes ago," he announced as he straightened, fairly dancing with excitement.

Riley narrowed his dark eyes as he stepped around his desk. Not much came over the Wallace Canyon PD fax machine. Mostly things meant for other fax machines that the sender had misdialed. "What is it?"

"It looks like an APB," Virgil said eagerly, finally moving fully into the doorway. "A regular manhunt."

Riley took a moment to note that there was no evidence of cookie crumbs on the deputy's uniform—identical to his own—of khaki shirt and trousers, but you never knew about some people. Although Riley's trusting nature had gotten him into trouble on more than one occasion, he decided to give Virgil the benefit of the doubt on this one. The man's agitation was clearly the result of the notice in his hand, and not some sugar-induced rush. Besides, Rosario, their receptionist-secretary-dispatcher was a notorious shortbread lover, herself. There was no end to the list of possible suspects.

"A manhunt?" Riley repeated, crossing the tiny office in a half-dozen long-legged strides.

Virgil nodded his head vigorously, his eyes sparkling. "Actually, it's even better. A *woman*hunt. And according to Rosario, the perp is right here in Wallace Canyon."

Riley shook his head slowly in bemusement. First cookie stealing, and now Virgil Bybee using the word *perp*. All in one day. Could his decrepit, thirty-two-year-old heart handle all this excitement?

He reached for the bulletin and quickly scanned it, then glanced back up at his deputy with as much patience as he could muster. "Virgil," he said quietly.

"Yeah, Riley?"

"She's not a perp. She's a missing person. And this is all old news. We got a fax about her...must've been a few weeks ago. I faxed 'em back and asked 'em to send me some more details, because Rosario told me she saw a woman here in Wallace Canyon who fit the description, but I never heard back so I figured they found her somewhere else. Looks like the fax machine's running a little slow. Again. This—'' he waved the paper in the air again ''—is evidently the details.''

Virgil gaped at him. "Old news? It's the first *I've* heard about it. There's been all this excitement goin' on, and y'all didn't even bother to *tell* me about it? Why am I always left in the dark this way? Why am I always the last person to know? Y'all never tell me anything around here.''

Riley rolled his eyes. "There was nothin' to tell, Virgil.'' But his deputy continued to pout, so, taking pity on him, Riley clarified, "The first time it came over the fax must've been back when you were in Guymon over Thanksgiving. A notice that this woman—'' He glanced back down at the fax in an effort to locate her name. "Sabrina Jensen,'' he said when he found it. "It said she was wanted by the Freemont Springs Police Department over there by Tulsa. But not because she's a perp, Virge. She's been reported as a missing person.'' He rattled the paper in his hand for emphasis. "It says so right here.''

The deputy's lower lip ceased thrusting out so much, but he was still obviously disappointed—probably because they wouldn't be calling out the hound dogs for a search. "Oh,'' he muttered. "I guess I didn't read that far. I just saw the part about her being wanted.''

Riley continued to read the notice, uttering his observations aloud this time, so Virgil could grasp more fully the reality of the situation. "Says Miss Jensen has been missing for months and is believed to be on the run. But this here's the part I can't figure out, Virge. The Wentworth family is looking for her. The Wentworths. And I just can't understand how she warrants that. I mean, they didn't even seem to know much about her before, but suddenly, I've got all this information. Now how do you figure that?''

"Should I know who you're talking about?'' Virgil asked. "Who are the Wentworths?''

Riley shook his head when he remembered where he was. "They're sort of famous-slash-infamous in that part of the state, but I can see how Wallace Canyon would have missed out on all the fuss.'' Hell, he could see how Wallace Canyon would have missed out on the Cuban Missile Crisis and that whole Tickle-Me Elmo thing.

Aloud, Riley continued, ''I know about them because I grew up just outside Tulsa. Big ol' oil family in Freemont Springs whose reputation, as they say, has always preceded them. Rich. Powerful. Pampered kids. That kind of thing. In fact, I had a run-in with the younger boy once, when he was drunk and disorderly at a frat party. Nothing major—just had to give him a stern warning. And I heard the older boy died—real recent, too, if memory serves—during some kind of explosion.''

''But this woman's name is Jensen,'' Virgil indicated unnecessarily.

Riley nodded knowingly. ''Yeah, and like I said, they didn't know that much about her when they sent that last fax. But suddenly, I now know that she's—'' he returned his attention to the fax and read word for word '''—Twenty-four years old, approximately five-foot-seven, medium build, dark brown hair, green eyes. All departments should be made aware—'''

His voice halted as he realized the answer to his own question was right there in black and white. ''Ah-ha,'' he said.

''Ah-what?'' Virgil asked.

''Looks like the reason there's all this sudden information about Miss Jensen is because she's been seein' an obstetrician who's just now comin' forward with the particulars of her situation.''

''An obstetrician?'' Virgil asked. ''Now, what difference would it make if she wears glasses or not?''

''No, Virgil,'' Riley groaned. ''Not an optometrist. An obstetrician. A doctor who delivers babies. Says here, and I quote, 'Ms. Jensen is also pregnant, due to deliver in—''' he glanced up at Virgil, paper held aloft ''—Where's the rest of it?'' he asked.

The deputy sheriff scrunched up his shoulders and let them drop. ''That's all that came over the fax,'' he said. ''Right after the photo of her.''

''Well, there should be at least another page,'' Riley stated. ''It's cut off midsentence here, and it doesn't even say why the Wentworths are looking for her.''

But Virgil was insistent. "I'm telling you, Riley, that's all that came over the fax."

Riley nodded again, sighing heavily. It had happened before. Like everything else at the Wallace Canyon police station, the fax machine was old, moody, unpredictable and in need of either a major overhaul or a total replacement—much like Wallace Canyon itself, he couldn't help but muse.

"All right," he finally conceded. "As long as we've got her photo and vitals, I guess this is enough to go on. Did Rosario see the photo?"

Virgil nodded. "Yup. That's why I said the perp...er, the missing person...is here in town. The minute Rosario saw that picture, she said that's definitely the woman she saw over in Westport. Then she went out to get some lunch."

Riley thought for a minute. "The only thing over in Westport is the trailer park."

Virgil's features wrinkled as he gave that some consideration, though why he should make such an effort, Riley couldn't imagine. "I don't think *trailer park* is the politically correct term, Riley," the deputy finally said. "I think they call them mobile home communities now."

First *perp* and now *politically correct.* What was Virgil reading these days? "Fine," Riley said. "There's nothing over in Westport except the mobile home community. That must be where Rosario saw her, 'cause that's where her sister lives."

Riley reached for the chocolate brown Stetson hanging on the coatrack near the door and settled it on his head, then shrugged a shearling jacket over his khaki uniform and began to button himself up. "Where's the photo of the woman?" he asked.

Virgil jabbed a thumb over his shoulder. "It's out on Rosario's desk."

"I'll take it and head over to Westport myself. Oh, and Virgil," he added as he passed by his deputy, "don't forget about those Lorna Doones. Because I sure as hell won't."

He wasn't sure if he imagined Virgil's seemingly heightened color or not, but Riley figured it never hurt to add a little emphasis. "Three o'clock," he repeated his earlier admonition. "I'll be back in the office by then, and those cookies better be waiting for me."

And with one final tug of the Stetson that brought it down low on his forehead, Riley turned and made his way toward Rosario's desk.

Rachel Jensen tossed a limp, wayward strand of tinsel back on the little plastic Christmas tree that squatted in her twin sister's rented picture window, and sighed with melodramatic melancholy. The single string of tiny, variegated lights wound around the tree flickered in an irregular rhythm, off and on, off... and...on...off-and-on, their flamboyant, if meager, celebration of color reflected on the window behind.

The view on the other side of the glass, however, was anything but merry and colorful. To the left, the flat, brown Oklahoma landscape stretched into oblivion beneath a thick, slate sky—not a hill or dale or tree in sight. Every few seconds a dry, fat snowflake interrupted the monotony, swirling up and around, dancing in the gusty wind that buffeted the rented mobile home.

Rachel had traveled all over the country with her truck-driving father, Frank, and her identical twin, Sabrina, from the time that the two girls were tots. But she'd never seen anything more predictable—or more boring—than the Oklahoma panhandle in the winter. Windy. Cloudy. Brown. Day after day. And now here it was, a little over a week before Christmas, and there wasn't a comfort or joy in sight.

"Merry daggone Christmas," she muttered to no one in particular.

She shifted her gaze to the right a bit, and was rewarded with a new sight for her trouble. The mobile home next door to Sabrina's was at least splashed with a bit of color, trimmed in yellow with a green front door, a scattering of plastic red geraniums swinging at regular intervals from its overhang. Having been in Wallace Canyon for less than two days, Rachel hadn't had the opportunity to meet any of Sabrina's rented neighbors. But at least one of them sure seemed to be fighting back against the landscape.

She ran a restive hand through her bangs, trailing her fingers back over her straight, dark brown, shoulder-length hair. Then she turned her back on the dubious vista outside Sabrina's window—not to mention on her sister's crummy excuse for a Christmas tree.

Had she not already known it, Rachel would have guessed that the mobile home to which her twin had summoned her was a rental, because it was furnished in traditional rental style—ugly. Brown furniture, brown paneling, brown carpeting, brown cabinetry...with a little tan and beige thrown in here and there for good measure. Rachel swore that if she ever got out of Wallace Canyon—and by golly, she *would* get out of Wallace Canyon, the moment she located Sabrina—she was never going to buy anything brown again.

But until that time came, it looked as though she was going to have to settle for lots of it. And that time wouldn't come until she figured out just where in the heck Sabrina was, how in the heck her sister had gotten herself into trouble, and what in the heck they were going to do to get her back out again.

Because being in trouble just wasn't Sabrina's style at all. Sabrina was the levelheaded one of the twin sisters, the one who had always been focused and certain, the one who knew exactly what she wanted and exactly how to go about getting it. Rachel was the one more likely to find herself *in* things. In dire straits, for example. Or in deep doo-doo. Or in hock. Or in over her head.

Sabrina, from all reports, had been doing great until recently. True, the two sisters weren't in touch the way they used to be—a two-hour drive one way tended to make it difficult for them to mesh their busy lives enough to get together in person. But they did speak pretty regularly on the phone. Up until a few months ago, Sabrina's life, by all accounts, had been full and active—and normal. She'd been working as a waitress and going to school at night, and she was *this* close to earning her degree in marketing. And she had all kinds of plans for after college, opening a chain of Route 66 diners that would no doubt make her a bundle someday.

Rachel, on the other hand... Well, even at the ripe old age of twenty-four, she still wasn't quite sure what she wanted to do with her life. Sabrina's dream of restaurants and franchises was a nice one, one she had envisioned for a long time now. But it was Sabrina's dream. Rachel wanted a dream of her own to chase after. She just didn't know exactly what it was yet. For the immediate future, though, it looked like her dream was to be stuck in Wallace Canyon, waiting for Sabrina to show up. And waiting. And waiting. And waiting.

The little community, for all its lack of variegation, animation, population and vegetation, was, nevertheless, Sabrina's last known location. Two nights ago, she'd called Rachel at her job in a bustling, rough-and-tumble Oklahoma City nightspot from this very mobile home. But Eddie, the bar manager, had caught Rachel behind the bar and on the phone in the middle of the conversation—and at the height of the after-work Happy Hour crush. Before Rachel had had a chance to find out the particulars of Sabrina's situation, he'd jabbed his thumb down on the button to cut the connection short. There had only been time for Sabrina to make Rachel promise to come to Wallace Canyon, to the Westport Mobile Home Community, where she was renting the mobile home on lot thirty-two, as soon as possible.

But when Rachel had arrived at the appointed address yesterday afternoon—losing her job in Oklahoma City in the process, because she'd been scheduled to work yesterday—Sabrina had been nowhere in sight.

The mobile home's front door had been unlocked, though, and nothing inside seemed to have been disturbed. There was evidence of very recent habitation—a six-pack of yogurt and half gallon of skim milk in the fridge—both far from expired—and some fresh fruit, not quite ripe yet, in a basket by the window. But there were no clothes in the drawers or closets, nothing to indicate that Sabrina had been the one living here. Upon checking with the manager, Rachel had learned that her twin sister had paid her rent through the end of the year—in cash. But Sabrina herself was nowhere to be found.

At this point, Rachel didn't know whether to stay or go. Whether Sabrina was hiding out nearby, was making her way back home to Tulsa, or had left Oklahoma entirely. All Rachel *was* certain about was pretty much what she'd been certain about in the beginning, a few months ago, back when Sabrina had first taken off. Squat. She was certain about squat. Except for the fact that her sister was in trouble. And alone. And on the run. And unwilling to tell anyone the particulars of her situation.

Oh, yeah. And she was pregnant, too.

Pregnant. Now that was another completely un-Sabrina thing for Sabrina to have done. If either of them had been voted by their senior class "Most Likely to Be Knocked Up and Abandoned," it was indisputably Rachel. Not that she slept around or anything like that. But she sure did tend to fall in love—and right back out again—way more often than the average woman did.

Just like her mother, she thought before she could stop herself.

As quickly as the realization erupted in her head, Rachel shoved it back down deep inside again. Instead, she reminded herself that it was Sabrina, not Rachel, who had found herself single and in a family way. Sabrina, not Rachel, who was on the run from some shadowy threat. It was Sabrina who'd landed in trouble this time. Now if Rachel could figure out where her sister was, then maybe, just maybe, the two of them could put their identical heads together and come up with a solution.

As had become an incessant habit over the last thirty-six hours, Rachel stared at the telephone affixed to the kitchen wall and mentally willed it to ring. Then, when mental willpower wasn't enough, she closed her eyes and started in on the customary verbal mantra that always followed.

"Ring, you stupid telephone," she whispered through gritted teeth. "Ring."

She had repeated the command four times when the telephone rang and scared the bejeebers out of her. "Hello!" she shouted into the receiver as she snatched it up, her entire body shaking.

"Rachel? Is that you?"

Rachel felt as if someone had come up behind her and hit her hard enough to drive the air right out of her lungs. For a moment, she couldn't breathe, couldn't speak. Then she gave her brain a good mental shove and cried, "Sabrina! Honey...where are you?"

"Thank goodness you're there," her sister began. Her voice sounded so distant, so faint and so scared that Rachel wanted to cry. "I tried you at your apartment first," Sabrina added, "and when you didn't answer, I hoped I could catch you at the trailer. And I'm sorry, but I can't tell you where I am."

"Of course you can tell me where you are," Rachel countered, knowing it was pointless. Although Sabrina had called her from time to time over the last few months, she'd never told Rachel where she was. Not until the other night, anyway. "I'm your sister for gosh sakes," she reminded her twin. "I've been worried out of my mind about you, and I don't know how much longer I can put off telling Daddy that you're in trouble."

"I can't tell you where I am," Sabrina repeated. "Because I'm only going to be here long enough to make this call. Then I have another bus to catch."

"*Another* bus?" Rachel echoed. "Sabrina..." For a moment, she let herself be overcome by the worry, the concern, the fear that had plagued her for months. "Sabrina, what on earth have you gotten yourself into?" she demanded. "All this secretiveness is making me crazy. When are you going to come home? Max said you used his address for mail for a bit, but that you never stayed there. So where have you been?"

There was a brief hesitation on the other end of the line, then Sabrina said, "I was in Mason's Grove for a little while, but I couldn't stay there."

"Where's Mason's Grove?"

"Between Tulsa and Stillwater. It's a real nice place, Rachel. You oughta visit there sometime. You'd like it."

They always did this. Started a conversation one way, branched it off to something else, then wound around to something else again. And somehow, they always kept track. Today, however, Rachel didn't feel like branching. Today, she wanted to stay on the topic at hand.

"Why didn't you call me or Daddy to tell us you were there?"

"I couldn't."

"Why?" Rachel repeated before expelling an exasperated sound. "Sabrina...honey, you've *got* to tell me what's going on. I mean it now."

"I wish I *could* tell you more," she replied, sounding as anxious as Rachel felt, "but it's just so complicated, and I'm not sure I know all the details myself, and I don't want to pull you into it, because it might be dangerous, and there's just not enough time, and..." She expelled an exasperated sound of her own. "Look, I just wanted to see if you were still at the trailer, and if you were, to tell you I'm not coming back, and you should leave. Do you hear me, Rachel? Leave. I don't think it's safe there."

"Oh, please," Rachel said. "What are you talking about? Not safe? This town is the most boring place I've ever been in my life. What could possibly be *not* safe here?"

She heard her sister sigh on the other end of the line. Then, in the background, a faint, disembodied voice dispassionately announced the departure of a bus to Lincoln, Nebraska.

"Is that yours?" Rachel asked. "Are you headed for Nebraska?"

"No. I'm going—" Whatever Sabrina had been about to say, she seemed to think better of it. "I can't tell you," she repeated.

"Why not? I'll meet you there. I'll call Daddy, and we can both meet you there. We can help you."

"Rachel, honey, there's something you need to know."

"Well, no doody, Sabrina." Momentarily, Rachel gave in to her frustration. "I think there's more than one thing I need to know. Like what exactly are you running from? Who the heck is the baby's father and why isn't he with you? Are you seeing a doctor? Are you eating right? Have you been taking your prenatal vitamins? Have I left anything out?"

Sabrina ignored her sarcasm. "All I can tell you is that I'm fine, and yes, I've seen a doctor—more than one, in fact—and everything is going perfectly according to schedule." After a clear hesitation, and with obvious reluctance, she added, "All I can tell you about the baby's father is that he comes from a very prominent Oklahoma family with a lot of money, a lot of power and a lot of influence, and..." There was another sigh, this one long and melancholy, followed by a softly uttered, "And...oh, Rachel. I think his family wants to take the baby away from me."

Rachel actually removed the receiver from her ear long enough to gape at it. Then she replaced it and exclaimed, "They want to *what?*"

"There's some guy following me," Sabrina continued in a

rush. "I don't know who he is or what he wants, but he's giving me the creeps. I think he might be working for Ja...for the baby's father's family, but whatever he's up to, it's no good."

"How do you know? Maybe he wants to help you."

"Trust me, honey. This guy isn't the helpful kind. He makes my skin crawl." After a brief hesitation, she added, "Someone broke into my apartment, Rachel, *and* tried to run me off the road. I think it's a safe bet that he was responsible for both. He's dangerous. And I won't risk having you and Daddy exposed to him."

"*What?*"

"Oh, I shouldn't have told you that," Sabrina said. "Look, I'm fine now. I'm safe. But I think I should keep moving."

"And *I* think you need to be with your family," Rachel countered. Shoot, Sabrina was going to give her a heart attack with all this woman-in-jeopardy stuff. "Sabrina, just tell me where you are, where you're going," Rachel pleaded. "I can meet you somewhere. It'll be okay with two of us. Even better, if I call Daddy, too. For heaven's sake, you're seven months pregnant! You need somebody with you!"

"No." Sabrina's tone of voice punctuated her adamant stance. "I'm fine. I knew the minute I hung up the phone the other night that it was wrong for me to call you in Oklahoma City. I was just feeling scared and alone, but I'm over it now. There's no reason to pull you into this, too. I'm on my own now. It'll be better that way. Go home, Rachel. Where it's safe. I'll call you when I can."

"But, Sabrina—" She stopped when another tinny-sounding departure announcement rang out in the background on the other end of the line. But the sound was muffled before Rachel could hear what it was, and she knew Sabrina had deliberately covered the mouthpiece of the phone.

When her sister came back on the line, it was to say quickly, "I have to go. Listen, just promise me you'll get out of there. And that you'll be careful."

"*I'll* be careful?" she repeated. "*I'm* not the one who's pregnant and on the run here—you are. *You* be careful. I can take care of myself."

Sabrina actually laughed at that. "Oh, yeah. Right. That's a good one, Rachel."

Rachel made a face at the phone. "Just tell me one last—"

"I have to go," Sabrina repeated. "I love you, Rachel. Tell Daddy I love him, too. I'll call you at your apartment when I can."

And then the buzz of a disconnected line hummed in Rachel's ear.

She stood there for a long time with the phone still pressed urgently to the side of her head, somehow feeling a little closer to her sister by doing so. Then an electronic female voice told her very politely that if she wished to make another call, to please hang up and try again. With a sigh, Rachel dropped the receiver back into its cradle, feeling worse now than she had when she'd first arrived at the rented mobile home in Wallace Canyon.

"Well, shoot," she muttered out loud. For good measure, she kicked the side of the kitchen counter with the toe of her heavy hiking boot.

There was no reason for her to stay here any longer. Sabrina had made it clear that she wasn't coming back, and whoever was following her was doubtless long gone from here, too. Rachel might as well just do as her sister had told her and go back home to Oklahoma City, where she could wait for Sabrina's next call. If there was a next call.

But something about going home rankled. Rachel didn't like feeling helpless, especially where her sister was concerned. There had been a time in the twins' lives when they'd been inseparable. Where one had gone, the other had followed, as if they'd been joined physically, as well as spiritually and emotionally. And although the leader had always been Sabrina—except, of course, for when the trail had led to trouble—Rachel had followed not out of obligation, but out of trust, out of love.

Sabrina had bailed her out of more tricky situations than Rachel could shake a stick at, and she'd never had the opportunity to return the favor. She *owed* her sister—big time. Now that Sabrina was the one in need of bailing out, the least Rachel could do was try to figure out some way to help. And sitting in her apartment back in Oklahoma City waiting for the phone to ring just wasn't going to cut it.

She leaned back against the wall, crossed her arms over the big, baggy, forest green sweater that hung nearly down to her denim-clad knees, cupped her chin resolutely in her palm, and wondered how on earth she was going to help Sabrina out when she didn't even know where her sister was headed. For long moments, she pondered her dilemma, until a brisk rap of a fist on the front door roused her from her thoughts.

Rachel snapped her head up at the intrusive sound, and riveted her gaze on the frosted glass of the aluminum door barely ten feet opposite her. Beyond it, she saw the silhouette of a big cowboy hat and little else. Something drew tight in her belly, and all her senses went on alert. She straightened, inhaled a few deep, fortifying breaths, and crossed to greet her—or rather, Sabrina's—visitor.

She gripped the doorknob carefully, inhaled again, then twisted and pushed slowly. But a gust of brutal winter wind snatched the door from her hand and sent it crashing outward, giving neither Rachel, nor her guest, a chance to ease slowly into things.

"Whoa," the cowboy hat said in response to the clatter of metal slapping against metal.

"Wow," Rachel gasped at the same time. Not because the wind had surprised her so, but because the cowboy hat tipped backward, and she got a good look at what was underneath.

More brown. But not ugly, dead-looking brown this time. Warm, animated, bittersweet chocolate brown, in the form of laughing eyes that gazed upon her with more than a little interest.

"Ma'am," the owner of those eyes said as he lifted two gloved fingers to the brim of his hat. "You okay?"

Rachel's mouth fell open, but no sound emerged. Instead, pretty much oblivious to the cold wind that bit through her sweater and tangled with her hair, she could only stare at the man on the other side of the door. Stare down at him, at that, because after knocking, he had retreated to the ground below the two metal stairs that extended from the side entrance of the mobile home.

His sunken position, however, did absolutely nothing to diminish him. He was easily six feet. And although his big, sheepskin coat hid the particulars of his physique, Rachel got the definite impression of solidity and strength. He was slim, sure, but no doubt every muscle he had, he made count.

Automatically, her gaze fell to the fourth finger of his left hand. It was a bartender's gesture she *always* performed, because men *always* flirted with female bartenders—even though they were often married when they did. This man's hands, however, were covered with rawhide gloves, so she couldn't be sure whether he wore a wedding band or not. Somehow, she found herself hoping he didn't. Then she shook her mind free of the thought and returned her gaze to his face.

Beautiful jumped into her head. He'd no doubt balk at being referred to in such a way, but that was the only word Rachel could come up with to describe him. His dark brown eyes were made darker still by the length of black hair that fell from beneath his Stetson, and by the two slashes of black eyebrows above and a ring of sooty lashes around each. His skin, too, was brown, a deep, smooth umber that was obviously a part of his heritage. His cheekbones were high and well-defined, his nose was straight and elegant, and they were complemented by a sensuously full lower lip that just begged to be tasted.

Oh, yeah. Definitely beautiful.

Great. Just what she needed. Rachel felt that old familiar falling sensation and knew that if she didn't pull back *right now,* she'd land in a puddle of ruined womanhood right at the man's feet. Nothing like falling completely in love with a man you've exchanged exactly one word with, she thought wryly. Nevertheless, she knew that was precisely what was happening to her now, because that was what always happened to her whenever she met an attractive man. So she commanded herself to knock it off, to rein herself in, to remember her sister and the fact that Sabrina had told her to be careful. And somehow, she managed to keep from throwing herself—body and soul—right into the beautiful man's clutches.

"Miss Jensen?" he said, sending a rush of heat right through her.

Shoot, heat was the last thing she needed, in spite of the frigid air buffeting her from all sides. When the man's voice finally registered in her muddled brain, she sensed by its tone that he must have uttered those two words several times without receiving an answer. Rachel shook her head hard again, to clear it of the muzziness that filled it, then forced herself to meet his gaze.

"Yes?" she replied, proud of herself for forming even that one-word in response.

"Sabrina Jensen?"

A faint alarm bell sounded in the back of Rachel's head, and for a moment, she felt like the proverbial deer trapped in the headlights of an oncoming semi. It certainly wasn't the first time someone had thought she was Sabrina, nor would it be the last. That was something identical twins just had to live with—mistaken identity. Normally, a brief, "Oh, no, I'm Sabrina's twin sister, Rachel," put a quick and painless end to the error.

But then, normally, Sabrina's questionable safety and bizarre recent behavior weren't at issue. Suddenly, with the up-in-the-air quality that Sabrina's life had adopted, Rachel's answer to the man's supposition now took on new importance.

She realized then that she had two choices. One, she could correct him, as she invariably did when one of her sister's friends or acquaintances mistook her for her twin, and then she and the cowboy hat could share a chuckle. Afterward, he could be on his merry way, and Rachel could go back to Oklahoma City, wait for Sabrina's call, and pray to God every night that her sister was safe and sound.

That, of course, was assuming that this man was a friend or acquaintance, which he probably wasn't, if he were asking her if she was Sabrina Jensen. If Sabrina had met this particular cowboy hat during her brief stint in Wallace Canyon, he'd realize right off the bat that there was something different about Rachel. Namely, the fact that she clearly *wasn't* seven months pregnant. In a word, duh.

So if this cowboy, however beautiful, *wasn't* a friend or acquaintance of Sabrina's, well then he might just be anybody. And *any*body could be *some*body who wanted to do Sabrina harm. After all, Sabrina had just told Rachel that Wallace Canyon wasn't safe. That someone was after her. That the someone in question had tried to hurt Sabrina and might potentially be trying to take her unborn child. Who knew who that someone might be? And he might not be working alone. It might just be a beautiful man with bittersweet chocolate eyes and a luscious lower lip.

Which brought Rachel to choice number two where mistaken identity was concerned.

She straightened, squared her shoulders and met those gorgeous brown eyes one-on-one. Then she told the man evenly, "Yes. I'm Sabrina Jensen. What can I do for you?"

Two

Riley Hunter had seen a lot of beautiful women in his time, but never one with eyes as clear and green and compelling as Sabrina Jensen's. A man could get lost in eyes like those, could gladly drown and never regret a second of his life. For a moment, he couldn't do anything more than gaze into those eyes and feel the world fall away from beneath him. Then the cold winter wind slapped him from the side, reminding him that he had a job to do.

"Forgive me, ma'am," he said, "but would it be all right if I came inside? It's fearsome cold out here today."

In response, Sabrina Jensen only stared at him in silence for a moment, as if she hadn't heard him, and he wondered if there was something wrong with her hearing. He'd had to ask her three times if she was Miss Jensen before she'd finally answered him. He was about to beg entry into the trailer again when, at last, she seemed to remember herself.

"Uh, no offense," she said, crossing her arms over her torso and tucking her hands under them in what had to be a totally pointless effort to ward off the cold. "But I'd just as soon we had our conversation right here."

He nodded, finally remembering that he had yet to introduce himself. Naturally, a woman wouldn't invite a strange man into her home. Deftly, he reached inside his coat and withdrew his identification. Unfolding the leather case, he held it up for her inspection. Her eyes widened at the sight of the silver star pinned to one side, then she reached out a tentative hand to pluck the entire case from his fingers.

She took her time reading over the laminated card that verified he was Sheriff Riley Hunter, Wallace Canyon PD, but even then, she evidently wasn't quite satisfied. She glanced first up at him, then back down at the photo, then up at his face again, then down at the photo. Sheesh. Talk about suspicious.

Riley wasn't used to having his identity or position in the community questioned, much less given this kind of scrutiny. Of course, even after only six months in residence, every single one of Wallace Canyon's 415 citizens knew him by name. He reminded himself that this woman was new to the community and living here alone, not to mention a woman who'd been reported missing—and a pregnant woman, at that. So he supposed she wasn't exactly in the position to be trusting. Still, it bugged the hell out of him to have his position, his very integrity, doubted.

As she studied his ID, his gaze involuntarily fell to her belly, which, even under her baggy sweater, offered absolutely no indication that there was a life growing inside her. She must be at the very earliest stages of her pregnancy, he thought. Although, like many men, Riley didn't know nothin' 'bout birthin' babies, even he suspected that a woman didn't go much beyond a few months before there was some sign of her condition. Miss Sabrina Jensen probably wasn't even out of her first—what did they call that thing again?—her first trimester. Yeah, that was it.

Even after she finished inspecting his ID and returned it, she studied his face for some time before she finally stepped aside to allow him entry. Immediately after Riley climbed the steps and crossed the threshold, she closed the door behind him. Then she wrapped her arms around herself again, as if closing the door on the wintry wind outside had done nothing to alleviate the fact that it was goll-danged cold. She didn't move away from the door, however, and somehow he decided that was because she wanted to be able to make a clean break of it, should he try anything funny.

Women. Man, they just couldn't trust anybody. And evidently, pregnant women were even worse. In an effort to assuage her fears, Riley took a few steps backward, until the opposite wall bumping into his fanny stopped him. Then, always the gentleman, he removed his Stetson, cradling it easily in one hand.

"Miss Jensen," he began again, raking his gloved fingers through his shoulder-length tresses to dispel any lingering effects of hat hair. Hey, a guy didn't want to look foolish when he was interrogating a beautiful woman, after all. "We received a report down at the station that identifies you as a missing person."

Two bright spots of color suddenly stained her cheeks, and Riley, whose instincts had always been right on the mark, immediately knew that she was guilty of either one of two things: either she was hiding something from him at the moment, or else she intended to hide something from him within the next few minutes.

But instead of calling her on it, he only waited to see what she would do. If there was one thing he'd learned as a law enforcement officer, it was that, nine times out of ten, if left to their own devices, people would do more damage to their own credibility than the police could ever hope to do. So Riley waited, feeding her all the rope she could possibly use in one lifetime to hang herself.

"A missing person?" she echoed, her voice more than a little tremulous.

"Yes, ma'am."

"But...but how could I be missing?" She scrunched up her shoulders and let them drop in a gesture that was way too quick and way too nervous even to be considered a member of the shrug family. "I'm right here."

Riley certainly couldn't argue with her logic. Nonetheless, he said, "Well, yes, ma'am, but you're missing from Freemont Springs, where an APB concerning your whereabouts originated."

"Now, how could I be missing from Freemont Springs?" she asked. "I've never even been there. I live in Oklahoma City and have for years."

"You're not living in Oklahoma City right now," he observed.

Again, that stain of color flooded her face. "Well...um, uh...actually..." Her voice trailed off, but her gaze never wavered from his. "Of course I'm living here *now*," she began again. "But until very recently, I was living in Oklahoma City."

Riley nodded. He didn't believe for a moment that she wasn't hiding something, but he nodded anyway. "And just what is it, pray tell, that brings you to our bustling little community?"

She swallowed visibly. "I, um...I needed to get away for a while. A, uh, a friend of mine who passed through here a while back told me what a great place this is, so I had to come and see for myself."

Oh, well, now he knew she was lying. "A friend told you Wallace Canyon was *great?*"

She nodded quickly, anxiously.

"That's like in that movie *Casablanca,* when Humphrey Bogart says he came to Casablanca for the waters, and then Claude Rains reminds him that Casablanca is in the middle of a desert, and it doesn't have any waters."

She narrowed her eyes at him. "Yeah. So. What's your point?"

His point was that she wasn't being truthful, but he checked himself before blurting that out. There were all kinds of things you could learn from a liar, after all. He'd seen that for himself. So aloud, he only said, "Well, to paraphrase Humphrey Bogart, ma'am, you were misinformed."

She cleared her throat indelicately. "That doesn't change the fact that I needed to get away for a bit," she said.

Again, her response seemed unlikely, and he didn't bother to hide his disbelief. "You needed to get away now?" he asked dubiously. "Right before Christmas?"

Still blushing, she nodded again, way too quickly for Riley's comfort. But she said nothing.

"Excuse me for doubting your word, ma'am, but seems to me this is the time of year when most folks want to be close to their loved ones, not get away from it all."

She lifted her chin a defensive fraction of an inch. "Yes, well, I think that probably depends on one's relationship with one's loved ones, doesn't it?"

He studied her in silence for a minute, unsure whether to believe her or not on that particular score. So he dropped that line of questioning and returned to his first. "That still doesn't explain why you've been reported missing. If not from Freemont Springs, then from Oklahoma City."

She gazed at him blankly. "Well, my goodness, Sheriff. Lots of people are missing from Oklahoma City. I'd venture to say that there are a lot of people out there who've never even visited Oklahoma City. If you have to round up everyone missing from Oklahoma City, then you better hurry and be on your way."

Ignoring her sarcasm, Riley said, "It's not my job to round up everyone missing from Oklahoma City, ma'am, only the people who've been *reported* missing. And the Wentworth family of Freemont Springs has reported you missing. It's my job to find you and let them know where you are."

She paused for a very telling moment before asking, "Who are the Wentworths?"

"Who are the Wentworths?" he echoed. Well, hell, she should know that better than him. She was the one they were looking for.

"I don't know anyone by the name of Wentworth," she said. "Sorry."

He sighed. "You've been living in Oklahoma City for years, and you don't know who the Wentworths are?"

She shook her head.

He wasn't sure whether or not to believe her on that score. The Wentworths were plenty famous in the state, but he supposed there were a good number of people who might not know about them, especially if they weren't Oklahoma natives. So, for now, Riley decided to play along, just to see how far Miss Sabrina Jensen was willing to play whatever little game she was playing.

"Wentworth," he repeated, enunciating the word a bit more clearly, a little more loudly, in case there really was something wrong with her hearing.

But she only continued to gaze at him tepidly, as if she had no idea what he was talking about.

So Riley continued, "Joseph Wentworth is a big ol' oil baron in Freemont Springs, which is not too far from Tulsa. Now, you do know where Tulsa is, don't you?"

Miss Jensen nodded, smiling eagerly. "Oh, yes. In fact, I have a—"

Abruptly, she stopped talking, her eyes widening in panic, as if she'd been about to reveal something she shouldn't. Riley waited to see if she'd continue, but she only snapped her mouth shut tight and said nothing more.

"You have a what?" he prodded her.

"Nothing."

"Oh, come on now, Miss Jensen, you were about to say you had a...what...in Tulsa?"

"A, uh..." she hedged. "An elderly aunt. Aunt Wisteria. She lives in Tulsa."

"Hoo-kay," he said. Might as well just get on with it. "The Wentworth family," he continued for Miss Jensen, "is real rich, and real famous—or maybe real *in*famous is a better way to put it. In any case, they're real popular, real well-known folks. They run Wentworth Oil Works. That ring a bell?"

In response, all Miss Jensen did was squint her eyes a little, as if she were immersing herself in thought, searching the data banks of her brain for the slightest inkling of familiarity. Riley shook his head at what he suspected was a monumentally fake effort, but continued on with his story in the hopes of jogging her memory—or wrangling the truth out of her—for what good it would do.

"Old Joseph Wentworth pretty much raised two grandsons and a granddaughter after their parents were killed in a boating accident, oh...years and years ago. They have a big, beautiful house in Freemont Springs. Rich folks, like I said. Powerful. Stand tall in the community. You following me?"

Another nod from Miss Jensen, but nothing otherwise.

"*Everyone* in that part of Oklahoma knows about the Wentworths," Riley continued. "Their activities are covered in the papers and on local TV *all the time*. I'd even wager to say that folks in Oklahoma City are pretty much aware of the Wentworths of Wentworth Oil Works in one way or another. Even the newcomers. Yet, you're telling me you've never heard of them?''

Miss Jensen's eyebrows arrowed downward as she processed this information—or at least pretended to. He was about to call her on her pretense when her expression cleared, and she lifted a hand to smack her open palm against her forehead. Hard.

"Oh, *those* Wentworths," she said.

Somehow, he managed to refrain from rolling his eyes. "Yeah. Those Wentworths."

"I'm sorry. I thought you were talking about some other Wentworths."

Other Wentworths, he muttered to himself. Yeah, right. "So you don't know the Wentworths personally?"

She shook her head.

"Well, the Wentworths sure know you. They're all het up to find you."

Sabrina Jensen shook her head. "I'm sorry, but I have no idea why they'd be looking for me. And as you can see, I'm perfectly fine, so..." She reached for the doorknob. "Will that be all, Sheriff?"

"Not quite."

She expelled an exasperated breath and tucked her hand back under her other arm. "I'm afraid I don't understand."

"That makes two of us."

Riley inhaled deeply as he studied Miss Sabrina Jensen's face again. Big mistake, he realized immediately. Because the moment he started looking at her, he found that he didn't want to stop. No woman should have eyes that beautiful, that compelling, that hypnotic. A woman could do a man serious damage with eyes like those. And this woman had clearly tangled intimately with at least one man recently, given the state of her womb. Who knew what she'd done to the poor sap?

Or what the not-so-poor sap had done to her.

Automatically, his gaze dropped to her left hand, where he saw no ring. Unmarried. Aha. It hit Riley then that maybe Miss Jensen was missing on purpose, because she didn't want to be found. *Especially* by the Wentworths of Freemont Springs, Oklahoma.

There was a father for that baby of hers out there somewhere, a father who hadn't yet married her. And Joseph Wentworth had a grandson. Even the older Wentworth boy might have fathered that baby before he died. Hell, for all Riley knew, maybe Joseph himself had a personal stake in finding Miss Jensen. Who knew what the particulars of her situation were?

"Miss Jensen," he began again, "do you mind if I ask you a few questions?"

"I thought you already had, Sheriff."

He nodded. "Yeah, but your answers to those only roused a whole bunch more that we need to talk about."

Without giving her time to answer, Riley settled his Stetson onto the settee beside him, tugged off his gloves and stuffed them into his coat pockets, then began to unbutton his coat. Miss Jensen opened her mouth to say something, seemed to think better of whatever it was, then closed it again. So he shed his coat and dropped it beside his hat, then he joined both on the settee and made himself comfortable. He slung his arm over the back, crossed his ankle over his knee, and met her gaze levelly.

Miss Jensen only stood staring back at him, as if she were trying to analyze him cell by cell. Those gorgeous green eyes of hers pinned him in place and held him there, assessing him, cataloging him, mesmerizing him. Riley began to feel as if he were a bug under a microscope, and Miss Sabrina Jensen was about to pick him apart. Then, thankfully, she sat down, too, in a chair positioned catty-corner to the settee.

"Can I fix you something to drink?" she asked halfheartedly. "Some coffee or something?"

He wondered for a moment if he should let on how much he knew about her, then decided that maybe she'd be more inclined to surrender information if she thought he already had most of it. So he replied, "I didn't think pregnant women were supposed to drink coffee."

The moment he said it, those two bright spots of pink appeared on her cheeks again, and her mouth dropped open in astonishment. Then she splayed her hand over her flat belly, as if she were trying instinctively to protect whatever life was growing there.

"You, uh, you know about that?" she asked.

He nodded. "It was in the latest APB we received about you. When are you due?"

Something—surely it wasn't relief—crossed her face, and she swallowed hard. "I, uh..." she began. But nothing more was forthcoming.

"Yes?" he spurred her.

But the only response she offered was another long, drawn out "Uh..."

"Miss Jensen?"

"Uh-huh?"

Hey, she was up to two syllables, Riley noted. Good for her. "You are pregnant, aren't you?"

She nodded quickly. "Uh, yes. Yes, I am."

Whoa, she was even using real words now, he thought. "When are you due?"

"In, uh, about, um..." She seemed to be thinking about something, then said, "June. I'm due in June. I'm three months along." To illustrate, she held up one hand, index, middle and ring fingers extended, as if she were a preschooler identifying her age. "This many," she said, enhancing the image. "Three. I'm three months. Yepper. That's how pregnant I am. Three months."

Riley nodded. Hoo-kay. Whatever. Nobody ever said beauty and brains went hand in hand, right? "Well, no offense, ma'am, but I'm not sure you're supposed to be drinking coffee. Not that I'm an expert or anything, but—"

"Oh, I'm not, either," she piped up. "An expert, I mean. This is my first time. Being pregnant, I mean. I'm sure the coffee is... I mean... Gee, I can't seem to stop saying, 'I mean,' can I?" She laughed, a nervous little trill that he found very suspicious. "I mean—oops, there I go again—ahem. That is to say—" She smiled, having conquered her problem by introducing a new phrase. "I *know* the coffee is decaf. Would you like some?"

He still hadn't quite recovered from the chill outside—or the prattling inside—so he nodded gratefully. Anything to give her something to do that would calm her down. But aloud, he only said, "Yes, ma'am. Thank you."

Even before he completed the sentence, Miss Jensen had shot

up from her seat and fled to the kitchen. Of course, seeing as how the kitchen was less than two feet away, it wasn't much of a flight. Strangely, Riley found that he was grateful for that, too. For some reason, he didn't want Sabrina Jensen out of eyeshot.

Of course, that was because she was part of a case right now, he assured himself—and *not* because she was just a good-looking woman he'd like to get to know better. He had no intention of getting to know her better. Not like that, anyway. Not...intimately. She was pregnant, for God's sake, something that tended to make a man think twice about involvement. For one thing, babies could put a real cramp in all that getting-to-know-you stuff. For another thing, it meant that she had a vested interest in another man.

Riley might have done some foolish things in his life where women were concerned, but he sure as shootin' wasn't about to infringe on another man's, uh...connubial jurisdiction. Of course, Miss Jensen was a self-professed *Miss,* reinforcing his suspicion that she wasn't married to whoever had sired that little nipper inside her, but still. The genesis of life tended to be a pretty major bond for people, didn't it? Even if the baby's father wasn't around, it was a good bet she still had fond feelings for the guy, and that the guy likewise still had a thing for her. Hey, baby or no baby, what man in his right mind would let a woman like Sabrina Jensen out of his sight?

"Aha," she said, bringing his attention around. When he looked up, he saw her standing in front of an open cabinet, a can of coffee in one hand.

"See?" she said, looking triumphant for some reason. "It *is* decaf. I told you so."

"Yes, ma'am," he replied, not sure why she should count the observation as such a coup. "You surely did."

She smiled as she closed the cabinet and moved toward the coffeemaker. And in spite of his earlier admonitions to himself, Riley found that he was more than a little interested in her movements. Everything she did was marked by a graceful efficiency and an easiness of motion that put his mind at peace. At least, her motions *were* efficient and easy—until she looked up and caught him watching her. Then all hell broke loose. The little plastic scoop full of coffee that she held in her hand went clattering onto the counter, scattering grounds everywhere, and when she scrambled to retrieve it, she bonked her head on the kitchen cabinet beside her.

"Ouch," she muttered as she lifted a hand to the injury. Unfortunately, it was the hand holding the coffee scoop, and she poked herself in the eye with it when she did.

"Ow," she muttered again.

"Here," Riley said, jumping up from the settee. "Let me help you." He did, after all, feel somewhat responsible for what had happened—he was the one who'd wanted coffee.

But the moment he took one step in Miss Jensen's direction, she leapt backward, an action that propelled her right into the refrigerator. Once again, her head snapped backward and bore the brunt of a blow, and he instinctively moved toward her, hands extended, in an effort to help her. But somehow his foot hit hers, and he, too, went sailing forward. By now, there were coffee grounds everywhere, Miss Jensen was suffering from a full-blown fit of embarrassment, and Riley wasn't sure what to do with his hands.

Ultimately, his hands took the decision, well, out of his hands, because they opted to land flat on the refrigerator door behind her, one on each side of Sabrina Jensen's head. And then the two of them stood quite literally face-to-face. And torso to torso. And libido to libido. And that was when the most bizarre thing popped into Riley's head.

He wanted to kiss Sabrina Jensen.

And that, he decided very quickly, would be a truly spectacular mistake. In spite of his decision, though, he couldn't quite bring himself to pull away from her just yet. Not because something in her eyes held him in thrall, and not because the heat of her surrounded him like a soothing balm, and not because she smelled just so damned good—like a field full of fragrant flowers.

But because she had dropped both coffee and scoop into the sink, and now she had her hands bunched fiercely in the khaki fabric of his shirt. Even more interesting, however, was the fact that instead of pushing him away—something he told himself any normal woman would do when faced by a complete stranger in such a way—she seemed to be pulling him nearer. Even *more* interesting was the way in which she was tilting her head back just a fraction of an inch, parting her lips as if she'd read his mind and, by golly, she wanted to kiss him, too.

"Uh, Miss Jensen?"

She had those luscious green eyes fixed on his face, and she seemed to be taking an inordinate amount of time studying each of his features. Though, when he got right down to it, Riley supposed she seemed to be most captivated by his...mouth? Uh-oh. They both really were thinking about the same thing, about how it would feel to—

"Uh, Miss Jensen?" he began again.

But she remained so preoccupied by her study of his face that all she offered in response to his query was a softly uttered "Hmm?"

He swallowed hard. "You, uh... Are you okay?"

Her gaze wandered over his features until her eyes finally met his. But again, all she managed in reply was a quietly murmured "Mmm."

He inhaled a deep breath and was immediately troubled by the shakiness of it. "Well, then, ma'am," he said softly, "would you mind letting go of my shirt?"

For a moment, he didn't think she'd heard him, and he wondered again about the state of her hearing. Then her eyes widened in surprise, her cheeks flushed that becoming shade of pink again, her lips parted more, as if she couldn't quite get enough air, and...

And she continued to hold fast to his shirt. So Riley circled her wrists with gentle fingers and, with no small effort, pried them loose. Only then did it finally seem to hit Miss Sabrina Jensen exactly what was going on. And it also seemed to hit her just how tenuous the situation was.

"Oh," she said softly. "Oh, dear. I am so sorry...."

She dropped her gaze to the hands he held in his and awkwardly yanked them free. Then, with quick, jerky movements, she began to smooth out the wrinkles in his shirt that her insistent grip had created. And at once, Riley wished he hadn't released her hands. Because the only thing more unsettling than having her fingers tangled in his shirt was having her fingers skittering lightly over his chest.

"I'm sorry," she said again, flattening her palms and pressing harder on his chest in an effort to iron out a few more places. "I have no idea how that happened. The coffee just slipped right out of my hands, and—"

Deftly, he caught her wrists in his hands again, and, startled, she glanced up into his eyes. For one long, lingering moment, he came *this* close to simply dipping his head to hers and kissing her, a good, solid, why-don't-we-just-dispense-with-the-formalities kiss, the way his instincts commanded him to. Then, somehow, he came to his senses and set her gently away.

"That's all right," he said, the words coming out a bit rougher than he'd intended. "Forget about the coffee. I'm not nearly as...uh...thirsty...as I was a few minutes ago."

Boy, that had been close. He'd almost told her he wasn't nearly as cold as he had been a few minutes ago, that being in close quarters with her had just heated him right up, and was she busy this evening, because he *really* wanted to get to know her and her hands better.

With no small effort, he forced himself to take a step backward in retreat. Then, somehow, he managed to take another. And then another. And another, and another, until he was as far away from Sabrina Jensen as he could be in the tiny confines of the trailer. Unfortunately, what stopped him was the entryway to her bedroom, something he discovered when his shoulder went slamming into the doorjamb, and he turned around to see what had impeded his progress.

"Damn," he muttered out loud when the sight of the small, intimate-looking bed had him spinning quickly back around. Trailers were just too damned small for a sheriff to be able to properly interrogate a beautiful woman. *Now* what was he supposed to do?

When he looked at Miss Jensen again, she didn't offer any answers. Instead, she was staring at him in a way that made his heart pound like a wild animal. Well, shoot. Nothing like being fiercely, irreversibly turned on by a total stranger, he thought. Especially one who was acting mighty suspicious about something and expecting another man's baby. What the hell was going on? Nothing like this had ever happened to him before. Hastily,

Riley reminded himself of all the reasons why he shouldn't be attracted to Sabrina Jensen.

Number one, she was pregnant. That was a pretty major reason in and of itself to keep his distance. But just to be sure, he heaped on a few more. Number two, in spite of that come-hither look in her eyes right now, she was probably in love with whoever had fathered her baby, another very good reason to avoid her. Number three, she'd been acting awfully funny ever since he entered the trailer—she obviously had something to hide. Number four, she'd lied about at least one thing, so who was to say she wouldn't lie about everything?

And number five, even without all of the above, Riley had sworn a *looong* time ago that it was going to take more than a beautiful face and a strong hormonal reaction to lure him into a relationship. When he started seeing a woman seriously again, it would be because she had wit, intelligence, integrity, honor and a strong sense of commitment. Miss Sabrina Jensen, so far, was showing signs of none of those things. And he'd be damned if he'd fall head over heels again just because of all that zinging of his heart strings. Hell, it had been bad enough when he was twenty-two, and Miss Caroline Merilee Dewhurst had—

He stopped himself before the memories of that ill-fated chapter of his life began to tumble into his brain. There was no reason to dwell on that right now, he told himself. Or ever again. Especially when the current chapter of his life was fast becoming a real page-turner.

"Miss Jensen," he said, trying again to jump-start the conversation, "would you mind coming down to the station with me so I can ask you a few questions?"

Her eyes widened in surprise again. "Am I under arrest?"

"No, ma'am," he was quick to assure her. "But I think the atmosphere at the station is a little more conducive to conversation than your trailer is."

"Conversation?" she echoed. "Sounds to me like you have something more along the lines of interrogation in mind."

He shook his head in firm denial. "No, I'd just like for you to clarify a few things for me is all."

"Then I'll clarify them right here."

Riley sighed. She was digging in. He could see it from a mile away. Miss Sabrina Jensen wasn't going anywhere with him today. "Fine," he told her. "Then I'll just give old Joseph Wentworth a call and let him know you're safe and sound and living right here in Wallace Canyon at the Westport Trailer Park, lot number thirty-two."

She narrowed her eyes at him. "They don't call them trailer parks anymore," she said. "This is a mobile home community."

He rolled his eyes. "Whatever. I think Mr. Wentworth will still be interested to know where you are."

Without waiting for acknowledgment, Riley moved gingerly over to the settee to retrieve his coat and hat, keeping Miss Sabrina Jensen in his peripheral vision at all times. Hey, you never knew. He had settled his hat on his head and was shrugging into his coat when she took a step toward him. But only one. It was as if she were as fearful as he was that getting too close would create something between them that they couldn't quite control. Like spontaneous combustion, for instance.

"Sheriff?" she said.

He finished buttoning himself up and looked at her. "Ma'am?"

"I'd really appreciate it if you wouldn't notify the Wentworths of my whereabouts."

That didn't exactly surprise him. "Why not?"

She lifted one shoulder and let it drop. "It's a long story."

"Well, then, why don't you come down to the station with me right now and tell me all about it? I don't have to be anywhere anytime soon. In case you didn't notice, Wallace Canyon is kind of a small town. Things are a bit slow here."

She nibbled her lower lip, as if she were trying to decide whether or not to come clean. And God help him, Riley decided he really, really liked how she did that. It made him wonder how it would feel to have those even, white teeth nibbling his lower lip, too. Not to mention some of his other body parts.

"I can't go into it right now," she told him, interrupting what had promised to be a very nice daydream. "I, um...I have a...a doctor's appointment. In...in thirty minutes. And I can't miss it."

"You gonna see Dr. Slater in town?" he asked, already knowing the answer. There was, after all, only one doctor in Wallace

Canyon, a general practitioner. The next closest one was an hour away and specialized in podiatry.

She nodded. "Uh-huh. Dr. Slater. That's who I'm seeing, all right. Ol' Doc Slater."

He eyed her warily again. "Dr. Slater is only forty-seven. And she really hates being called 'Doc.'"

Her eyes widened. "Oh. I see. It, uh...it's my first appointment."

He nodded, but still felt that edge of suspicion twisting up his spine. "Okay. Then you can come by the station after you're finished. You know where the station is?"

She nodded again. "Sure. Sure I do."

"Then I'll see you in about an hour?"

She licked her lips. "Uh...better make it an hour and a half," she said.

He nodded. "I'll see you then, Miss Jensen."

"Yeah. Okay. Fine. Whatever."

For some reason, she seemed to be awfully worried about something. Then again, being summoned to the police station, even for something as minor as questioning, probably roused more than a few concerns in a person.

"I look forward to having my questions answered," he said, lifting two gloved fingers to the brim of his hat in farewell.

And then Sabrina Jensen said the strangest thing in response. "Yeah. I will, too."

Three

——

Rachel closed the door on Sheriff Riley Hunter, Wallace Canyon PD, bolted it as quickly as she could, then leaned against it with all her might. Somehow, she hoped doing so might keep all her problems at bay, and keep all of her lunch in her stomach. But even after shutting her eyes and taking ten deep breaths, even after silently uttering her favorite daily affirmations, even after that...that...that whattayacall...that visualization thingy where she tried to see herself floating peacefully on a raft in the middle of a swimming pool...

She sighed deeply. Even after all that, she was still shaking like a jackhammer, and her stomach was still rolling. Her legs finally buckled under her, and she slid slowly down along the door until she'd crumpled in a heap on the floor. Then she buried her face in her hands and bit back a groan.

She'd just told a pack of lies to a police officer! A really cute one! Now what was she going to do? More to the point, what on earth would bring a really cute police officer to Sabrina's mobile home in the first place? Why were the illustrious Wentworths of

Freemont Springs looking for her, to the point of siccing the police on her?

Rachel covered her mouth with a loose fist and replayed the scene that had just transpired between her and Sheriff Gorgeous, feeling sicker and more confused with every passing moment. Could one of the Wentworth grandsons be the father of her sister's baby? she wondered. If so, it would answer at least a few of the questions spinning around in Rachel's muddled brain. Hadn't Sabrina just said on the phone that the baby's father came from "a prominent Oklahoma family," one that had a lot of money and power and influence? And Sabrina lived in Tulsa, not far from Freemont Springs at all. It was certainly possible that she had crossed paths with one of the Wentworths.

That had to be it, Rachel thought. That was the only explanation that made any sense. Somehow, Sabrina must have become romantically involved with one of the Wentworths, and had gotten pregnant as a result of the relationship. And now, evidently, the Wentworths had found out about the baby, and they were looking for the baby's mother.

Boy, the twin sister was always the last to know.

Then Rachel remembered something else her sister had said on the phone. That the baby's father's family was trying to take the baby away from her. Oh, no. Oh, jeez. Oh, man. No wonder Sabrina was on the run. No wonder she was hiding out and didn't want to tell anyone where she was. Just what had Sabrina gotten herself into?

And just what had *Rachel* gotten herself into? Not only was she now a part of this whole thing, but she'd just lied to the law like a big dog. That was probably illegal, and was certainly immoral. And no doubt ineffective to boot, because she was a terrible liar, always had been, always would be.

Hoo boy, was she in it now. Deep.

It was just that she hadn't known what to do. Even on her best day, when she *wasn't* worried sick about her sister's welfare, Sheriff Riley Hunter was the kind of man who would send Rachel into a tailspin. For Pete's sake, he'd been *sooo* handsome. And charming. And sexy as all get-out. The moment he'd entered Sabrina's trailer—or rather, mobile home, she corrected herself—

he'd taken over the place, filling it physically, spiritually, completely. And Rachel just hadn't known what to do. So she blithered like an idiot, told one lie after another, and confused herself so badly that now she had no idea what to do.

She blamed her instincts, which were in no way reliable. Her first instinct had been to protect Sabrina and the baby at all costs—which, now that she thought about it, had probably been a pretty good reaction to have. But her second instinct had been to play her hand close, to feel the sheriff out and see what kind of light he might shed on the situation. Which, too, now that she thought about it, probably hadn't been such a bad thing to do, either, all things considered.

So it must have been her third instinct that had tripped her up, the one that had urged her to keep mum about her own nebulous part in whatever was going on. Which, on second thought, hadn't really been all that dishonest, because she didn't know what was going on anyway.

Okay, so maybe her instincts weren't *that* unreliable, after all, she amended. Still...

She really hadn't known what was going on, she tried to reassure herself. Not when she'd started lying anyway. And by the time she'd begun to get some kind of fuzzy picture regarding Sabrina's situation, she'd been too far gone into Fabrication Land to find her way back. And now, even though things were starting to fall into place, she wasn't altogether certain that she *should* start telling the truth. The father of Sabrina's baby appeared to be a member of one of the most powerful, most influential families in the state. And evidently, they wanted possession of that baby, to the point of bringing in the law.

Contrary to the act she had attempted to play with Riley—however badly—that she'd never heard of the Wentworths, Rachel, like everyone else in Oklahoma, knew *exactly* who they were.

Who knew what motivated them, or what lengths they would go to to get their hands on Sabrina's baby? Who knew who they had on their payroll, or how successful they'd be in their efforts? Oh, sure, they seemed like a nice enough family—on the outside, at least—from what scraps of gossip and chitchat she had heard about them over the years. But the Wentworth kids had been in and out of minor trouble a lot, too, from what she'd also heard over the years. And who could tell what people were capable of? Especially rich people. They always acted as if they were above the law.

Or, at least, Rachel *assumed* that rich people always acted as if they were above the law. That was what she'd always heard, anyway. She didn't actually know too many rich people herself. Or any, for that matter. Still, one heard stories about such things. As far as she knew, the Wentworths might very well be manipulating the legal system, and who knew what—or who—else, to further their own interests.

They might very well be looking for Sabrina just so they could take her baby away from her. They had money and resources, and no doubt friends in high places, where Sabrina had nothing but a bartender sister and truck driver father and a dream of self-employment that was anything but fulfilled. If the Wentworths decided to take her baby away from her, they could probably find some way to do it. Hey, it could happen. From outward appearances, they had far more going for them than Sabrina Jensen did.

At this point, Rachel simply did not know what to think or what to do. Without meaning to, she had become involved in this thing, almost as much as Sabrina was. All she could do now was try to see it through to the end, until Sabrina and her baby were assured a lifetime of love and safety and togetherness. Whatever she had to do to ensure that for her twin, Rachel would do it. Even if it meant lying to a cute sheriff. It was for a good cause, right? The ends justified the means, didn't they?

So then, why did she feel so guilty for what she had done, for what she was about to do?

She pushed the thought away and herself up off the floor, then made her way to Sabrina's front window. She glanced out just in time to see Sheriff Riley Hunter's big utility vehicle—brown again, wouldn't you know, with a beige star painted on the door—turning out of the trailer park...er, mobile home community...and onto the highway. Then she took a deep breath, raked both hands slowly through her dark hair, and reassessed her predicament.

Nothing was going to change the fact that she had just lied to a police officer, so she was just going to have to deal with that. And there was still that small matter of her having agreed to meet with said police officer at the station in an hour and a half, something Rachel was sure she wouldn't be able to avoid. Not unless she grabbed her bag and returned to Oklahoma City, where she would be totally ineffective in helping Sabrina. If Rachel didn't go down to the station as she'd promised, then Riley Hunter and his beautiful brown eyes and lush lower lip would just come back to the trailer park—er, mobile home community—to find her. Or worse, he would call the Wentworths and bring them into the whole sordid mess.

So she figured she had two ways she could go. Either she could meet with the sheriff as she'd promised and come clean with the truth—that she was really Sabrina's twin, who didn't have a clue what was going on or where her missing sister might turn up, and sorry about all those whopping fat lies. Or she could keep perpetuating the whopping fat lie that she *was* her missing sister Sabrina, in the hopes of learning a little bit more about the situation, and a little bit more about the good sheriff's intentions.

If Riley Hunter was indeed nothing more than a small-town lawman who'd been pulled into this thing as innocently as Rachel had been, then maybe, eventually—once she knew she could trust him—the two of them could put their heads together and find Sabrina.

On the other hand, if Riley Hunter was a hired gun of the Wentworths who was supposed to find Sabrina and return her to Freemont Springs for the Wentworth's nefarious intention of taking her baby away from her, then posing as Sabrina might buy her sister some time and throw her pursuers off her trail.

Because really, when Rachel got right down to it, just who was Sheriff Riley Hunter anyway? How was she supposed to tell whether he was a legitimate man of the law or the mysterious someone that Sabrina said was after her? Oh, sure, he was cute and everything, and he'd been totally polite and sweet, and it had just been so heart-melting, the way he'd kept calling her "Ma'am," and—

Rachel stopped herself before her capricious heart had the two of them walking down the aisle to the "Wedding March." It was bad enough that she'd almost kissed the man a few minutes ago. *Kissed* him, she recalled with mortification. This, when she didn't even know if she could *trust* him. Honestly. No woman on earth was as weak-willed as she was when it came to the opposite sex. She didn't even know who the heck Riley Hunter was, and already she was half in love with him. And that wasn't going to do Sabrina one whit of good. Or her, either.

Be strong, Rachel, she commanded herself. *You can ignore beautiful brown eyes and a lush lower lip. You can avoid going all gooey inside every time you hear him say, "Ma'am" in that smooth, deep, utterly masculine voice of his. Just remember Sabrina. And don't look at Sheriff Riley Hunter unless you absolutely have to.*

Okay, she finished up her little pep talk to herself. She could do this for Sabrina. She could pretend to be her pregnant twin, especially since Riley Hunter obviously didn't know that Sabrina was seven months along, and thank goodness for that.

She squared her shoulders, inhaled a deep breath and expelled it in a rush of certainty and good intentions. Just this once, Rachel wanted to be the twin who did the right thing. Just this once, she wanted to be the one who got them *out* of trouble, instead of into it. Just this once, she'd like to do something to help out Sabrina, the way Sabrina had always been doing something to help out Rachel. Just this once, she needed to do something right.

Please, she begged anyone who would listen. *Just this once, let me get it done right.*

If she hadn't been looking for it—or if she had blinked—Rachel would have completely missed the Wallace Canyon police station. A tiny brick storefront tucked in between two other tiny brick storefronts—Wanda's Wonderful World of Hair, and Fern and Moody's Uptown Diner—the station was hardly noticeable. Even the words stenciled on the glass door that identified it were old and faded, nearly indecipherable, punctuated as they were by a jagged crack that bisected them. With red-mittened hands, Rachel pulled the collar of her down coat more tightly around her throat, tugged her red knit cap more snugly over her ears, then turned the knob and entered.

On the other side of the door, she found a tiny, cramped room, furnished in early Eisenhower era. Dulled yellow linoleum covered the floor, and orange plastic chairs lined one faded gray wall. A minuscule Christmas tree sat on a table in one corner, strung with garland and not much else. To its right was another table set up with a coffeepot and various condiments, few of them having anything to do with coffee.

At first, Rachel thought the place was deserted. Then, gradually, she noted evidence of life. Straight across from her was a desk, a handful of papers scattered across its surface, a dilapidated lamp at one corner casting a spastic beam of white light over the clutter. Behind the desk crouched a rickety metal chair with wheels, its seat obscured by a lumpy cushion, a woman's sweater slung over the back. On a nearby shelf, a radio crackled with a nasally rendition of an old country-and-western ballad. But there wasn't a living soul to be seen anywhere.

Evidently, *someone* worked here, Rachel thought. Now if she could just locate the person who—

"Miss Jensen."

She whipped her attention to the left and saw Sheriff Riley Hunter sauntering through a door, hand extended, an easy smile softening his already gentle features. And immediately, all of Rachel's earlier convictions about being able to carry off her deception began to crumble. Because he was still gorgeous, still charming, still sexy as all get-out...and she still wanted to kiss him senseless.

Daggone it.

"I'm glad you could make it," he said as he continued forward. "And you're even a few minutes early."

"Sheriff," she managed to say, troubled by the light tremor that shook her greeting. Automatically, she tugged off one mitten and lifted her bare hand to place it in his. His skin was warm and rough, his grip firm, his hand twice the size of her own. And she realized that, like the rest of him, his hands were simply too irresistible for words.

She scrambled to remember what they were supposed to be talking about. Oh, yeah, she quickly recalled. She had been about to feed him another pack of lies.

"Of course I made it," she said, her voice still sounding wobbly. "Did you doubt that I would come?"

"Oh, no, ma'am," he rushed to assure her, hooking a hand on each hip in a way that she simply could not ignore.

Goodness, but he had nice hips. Hands. She meant hands, not hips. She would never notice a man's hips. Never. She wasn't that kind of girl. It was Sheriff Hunter's hands that were nice. Hands. Of course. Ahem.

"But sometimes," he continued, bringing her thoughts back around, "those doctor's appointments can go on a bit longer than you might think they would."

"Yes, well…" *Not if you didn't go,* she thought. Aloud, she said, "About those questions you wanted to ask me…?"

He nodded. "Would you mind coming back to my office?"

Mind? Of course she'd mind. "Not at all," she said.

He led the way down a short hall that was as deserted as the rest of the place seemed to be, and Rachel made every effort to *not* notice his hips again. She also found herself wondering just how many people made up the Wallace Canyon Police Department. Sabrina certainly had gone out of her way to choose a spot that was out of the way. Why hadn't she just remained here? No one could have found her here. Tiny, desolate Wallace Canyon seemed to be the perfect hiding place.

Except, of course, for the fact that someone *had* found Sabrina here. Oh, hey, but other than that—

"Miss Jensen?"

Too late, she discovered that Sheriff Hunter had stopped walking and was gesturing into an office that was as small, badly lit and empty as the rest of the place seemed to be. Unfortunately, that particular discovery was one she made right after running her body right smack into his, because as she'd been sizing up his office, he'd halted to let her enter first. And then, just as she had less than two hours before, she found herself once again surrounded by Riley Hunter. Surrounded by his heat, his scent and his rather extreme masculinity.

"Oh," she murmured, instinctively moving her hands up to steady herself. And, just as they had before, her traitorous fingers curled themselves into the stiffly starched khaki fabric of his shirt.

And just as Riley Hunter had before, he circled her wrists capably with his warm, rough fingers, and withdrew her hands from their nesting place. But, again, he didn't quite let her go. When Rachel glanced up at his face, his dark eyes were alive with the glitter of something she didn't dare ponder, something that made her heart race quadruple time.

"Ma'am?" he said, his voice rougher, huskier than it had been.

"Yes."

Rachel's one-word reply was a statement, not a question, because at that point, she realized that whatever Sheriff Riley Hunter asked her to do, she would do it, gladly and without second thought, and never regret for one moment whatever it was.

"You want to go into my office?" he asked. This time he punctuated the question by releasing one of her wrists and jabbing a thumb over his shoulder, toward the interior of the room, which she duly ignored.

"Yes." But in spite of her affirmative response, Rachel didn't move from her position.

"We'd have a bit more privacy in there."

"Yes." Still, neither of them moved.

"You could sit down."

"Yes."

"I imagine a woman in your condition tires pretty easily, huh?"

"Yes."

"I...uh...I don't have a lot to offer in the way of refreshments, but I think I could scrounge up a couple Lorna Doone cookies. How would that be?"

Although it wasn't exactly the offer Rachel had been expecting to hear, she answered all the same, "Yes."

He nodded.

And she reiterated, "Yes."

And then they just stood still, looking at each other some more. Slowly, it dawned on Rachel that the way Riley Hunter was staring at her wasn't quite the same way she was doubtless staring at him. While there was no question in her mind that she was studying him with what pretty much amounted to, oh...she didn't know...perhaps an intense, feral, voracious lust...he was studying her with what pretty much seemed to be, um...well, concern, really. As if he were worried about, oh, say, her sanity, for instance.

And that was when it hit her that although there was unquestionably an electricity arcing between the two of them, that electricity wasn't quite reaching Sheriff Hunter.

"Yes," she said, one final time, in spite of her recognition of the one-sidedness of the attraction. Then, somehow, she managed to add, "Thank you. I'd love a couple of Lorna Doones. They're my favorites."

She wasn't sure, but for a moment, Riley Hunter seemed to be regarding her with a fair amount of suspicion—even more suspicion than he'd shown in Sabrina's trailer. Or, rather, Sabrina's mobile home. Then, just as quickly as his expression had grown troubled, it cleared, and he tilted his head to the side, toward the interior of his office.

"Make yourself comfortable," he said. "I'll see if I can't wrangle up some milk to go with those cookies. You being in your condition and all, you could probably use it."

Rachel nodded, but he didn't hang around long enough to see it. Instead, he bolted down the hall. She sighed as she watched him go, then removed her other mitten, unsnapped her coat and strode into his office, making herself at home in a battered, pea green, Naugahyde chair that sat opposite his desk. It was a remarkably ugly piece of furniture, she noted as the chair squeaked beneath her svelte build. But at least it wasn't brown.

"Here you go, Miss Jensen."

Sheriff Hunter's voice interrupted the uncomfortable silence, and she turned to see him entering with a coffee mug and napkin, which he settled on his desk within arm's reach of her. Once he seated himself behind his desk, he opened a bottom drawer and withdrew a box of cookies, which he also pushed toward her, so that she had simply to reach out to serve herself.

Obviously, he didn't want to be within touching distance of her, she noted. Which, now that she thought about it, was probably a good thing. Because she was none too eager herself to repeat that embarrassing display of...of...of whatever it was that they'd displayed for each other earlier.

"Now then," he began when he'd made himself comfortable. He drove one hand through that black silky curtain of hair, then wove his fingers together on his desk. "Why don't we just cut to the nitty-gritty, and you tell me how you came to be involved with the Wentworths."

Rachel had removed a cookie from the box, but dropped it onto the napkin as her appetite evaporated. "I told you—I don't know the Wentworths. Not personally, anyway."

"Then why would they have had the Freemont Springs police put out an APB on you, reporting you as a missing person?"

She tried to console herself that, for now, at least, she had the opportunity to tell the truth. "Honestly, sheriff, I don't know," she said.

He eyed her thoughtfully for a moment. "I ran a check on you after I left your trailer earlier." He held up a hand when she opened her mouth to correct him. "Your mobile home," he said impatiently. "But nothing interesting came up. Not so much as a parking ticket."

"You ran a check on me?"

Rachel wasn't sure what bothered her more. The fact that he'd mistrusted her enough to run a check on her—even though she *had* been lying and, therefore, hadn't been particularly trustworthy—or the fact that there was nothing interesting on her permanent record. A girl liked to have *some* kind of mystery in her past, after all, *some* kind of questionable black mark.

Then she remembered that he would have been checking into Sabrina's past, not Rachel's, and she heartened some. *Of course* there wouldn't be a blot on Sabrina's permanent record. Sabrina had never done anything wrong. Well, not until recently, anyway. Not until she'd gotten herself knocked up with the heir to one of the wealthiest, most prominent, most powerful families in Oklahoma, who wanted to take her baby away from her, thereby forcing her to go on the run. But surely there was a black spot on *Rachel's* record, *some*where in her past. She could dream, anyway.

"No offense, Miss Jensen," Sheriff Hunter said, interrupting that dream, "but running a check like that is standard procedure.

I just wanted to rule out the possibility that you might be wanted for something other than being a missing person.''

Rachel lifted her nose haughtily into the air. "I beg your pardon. I have *never* broken the law.'' Lied to a police officer, okay, she qualified to herself, but broken the law? Never. Not unless, of course, lying to a police officer was against the law, which, now that she thought about it...

Uh-oh.

"Yes, ma'am. If you say so.''

She stood quickly. "May I go now?''

The sheriff shook his head, and waved his hand in a silent motion for her to sit back down. Rachel sighed as she did so, then reached for her cookie, more to have something to do with her restless hands than because she was really interested in eating anything.

"So, if you don't know the Wentworths,'' he began again, "then why are they looking for you? You can tell me, Miss Jensen. I'm a very understanding, very reasonable, person. I promise.''

Rachel nibbled fitfully on her cookie, sipped milk from the mug and remained silent. There. Let him interpret her lack of a response however he wanted to.

Evidently, he wanted to interpret it as her hiding something, because he moved his hand to place it on top of the telephone perched at the corner of his desk. "If you won't tell me, Miss Jensen, then I have no choice but to call the Wentworths right now and tell them that I have you in my possession.''

Ooo. He had her in his possession. Rachel kind of liked the sound of that. For a few seconds, anyway. Then she remembered that being possessed by Sheriff Riley Hunter—in *any* way—was the *last* thing she needed. She gave herself a good mental shake and commanded herself to stop being so moon-eyed over someone she might not even be able to trust.

Reaching across his desk, she covered his hand with hers and said softly, "Please, don't.''

He said nothing for a moment. Nor did he remove his hand from where he'd rested it. Instead, he only leveled his gaze on her face as he thought long and hard about something. Then, finally, he said, "Give me one good reason why I shouldn't call them. Otherwise, I'll make sure you sit tight until they get here, and, knowing them, that won't take more than a few hours."

Rachel sighed. It was now or never. She either had to come clean with the truth of her identity, or commit herself to perpetuating a falsehood that would likely land her in *biiig* trouble. Still, however, she hesitated.

"One reason, Miss Jensen," he repeated in that smooth, level tone of voice. "That's all I need."

"All right," she finally conceded. "I'll give you one reason. Because...because I haven't exactly been honest with you."

Sheriff Hunter arched his eyebrows in question but didn't release the phone. So Rachel curled her fingers more resolutely over his warm, rough flesh and continued.

"I...I really do know the Wentworths," she said. Okay, so she was lying to him about lying to him. Or something like that. It was for Sabrina and her unborn baby, right? "I know the Wentworths, and...and I'm hiding from them. On purpose. You can't tell them you've found me."

"Is one of the Wentworth boys the father of your baby?" he asked bluntly.

Still preoccupied by thoughts of Sabrina, and before she realized how her answer would be interpreted, Rachel blurted out, "I don't know."

This time, in addition to his eyebrows arching, Sheriff Hunter's mouth dropped open. "You don't know?" he repeated. "You *don't know* if one of the Wentworths is the father of your baby?"

"Uh..." Rachel began eloquently. She scrambled for an explanation that wouldn't make her sound immoral, careless, promiscuous or stupid. "It's just that, um..."

"Yes?"

"Well, one of the Wentworth boys *could* be the baby's father. Probably is, in fact."

"*Could* be? *Probably* is?"

"Or...or...or it could be someone else," she finished lamely.

Oh, nicely done, Rachel, she congratulated herself. No way did that answer make her sound immoral, careless, promiscuous, or stupid. No, that response had made her sound immoral, careless, promiscuous *and* stupid. Duh.

"Well, which one of the Wentworths is in the running?" the sheriff asked, his voice a bit strained when he did.

And again, worried for Sabrina, and without thinking, Rachel replied honestly, "I don't know."

Immediately, she squeezed her eyes shut tight at what she had just implied with her ill-spoken response. That she had been intimate with *both* of the Wentworth brothers. Oh, and, of course, with someone *else* who might potentially be the baby's father.

Great. This was just great. She'd just led a cute sheriff to believe that she'd been sexually involved with three men within the last few months. For heaven's sake. Rachel hadn't even had three *dates* in the last few months, let alone been intimate with anyone. For that matter, she hadn't even had three lovers in her *entire life*. What must the good sheriff be thinking of her right now?

When she opened her eyes to brave a glance at him, he looked as if he wanted to hit something. Hard. "Just how many men are in the running for having contributed that second set of chromosomes, Miss Jensen? Would you mind telling me that much, at least?"

Rachel licked her lips, opened her mouth to say something, decided that doing so would probably just get her into deeper doo-doo, and closed it again. For one long moment, she thought hard about how to answer that question without having to backpedal and make herself sound even more careless, more immoral, more promiscuous and more stupid than she already had. Finally, she decided to go with, "Three. There are, uh...three possible candidates for, um, for fatherhood. The Wentworths, and, uh, this other guy."

Sheriff Hunter, whose hand, Rachel noted, still rested on the telephone, watched her in silence for some moments, as if he were trying real hard to figure her out. Good luck, she thought. She was still trying to figure herself out. She couldn't imagine what had come over her to lie like this and paint herself in such a dubious manner. It was one thing to protect one's twin sister from a perceived danger. It was another thing entirely to put oneself in the position of looking like a total doofus.

"So you see, Sheriff," she began again when her companion remained silent, "I'm in something of an awkward position where the Wentworths are concerned."

"Yeah, you're in a position, all right," he conceded with a less than polite expulsion of air. "Matter of fact, it sounds like you've been in a lot of positions lately." Before Rachel could utter a single word in objection, he hurried on, "Just what exactly you might call your current one, however... Now that's the big question, isn't it?"

Although she was tempted to smack that disapproving expression from his face, Rachel ignored his sarcasm and innuendo and said, "Please don't tell the Wentworths you've found me. Just give me some time—say, a week—to sort things out. Then, I promise, I'll go to them myself and tell them what I can about my situation."

That, at least, Rachel vowed to herself she would do. If she couldn't figure out where Sabrina was or what she was doing in one week's time, or if she hadn't heard from her sister about what—or what not—to do, then Rachel would go to the Wentworths and try to make some sense of this whole thing. She promised herself that. And she promised Sheriff Hunter again, too.

"I promise," she repeated. "Just give me a week to figure things out."

"A week," he echoed. "And do you really think you'll figure it out in that length of time? This whole thing sounds mighty complicated to me."

She nodded. "A week is all I need. Surely it's not going to cost you anything to give me a little time."

He eyed her thoughtfully. "How do I know you won't take off again and disappear the minute you're out that door?"

Rachel eyed him back, hopefully. "You, uh, you have my word?" she said in a very small voice. Oh, yeah. That ought to convince him.

He uttered that impolite sound again and frowned at her. "Forgive me, Miss Jensen, but I don't think I know you well enough to accept your word, and frankly, you haven't been the most honest person in the world since I met you all of two hours ago."

She supposed she'd had that coming. Still, it hurt to realize that he had deemed her so untrustworthy. Even if she hadn't been exactly, well, trustworthy.

"No offense taken, Sheriff," she said softly. "But I don't know what to tell you to convince you. Look at it this way. I'm trusting you not to call the Wentworths for a week. Why can't you trust me not to run off?"

"I suppose you've got a point there," he ceded with obvious reluctance. "Still..."

"I promise you I'll stay put at the trailer—er, mobile home...oh, what the heck, at the trailer—for one week, if you'll promise me that you'll wait one week to call the Wentworths. Please. I'm begging you."

Again, he studied her in silence, and Rachel wished with all her heart that she could see into his brain and find out what he was thinking. Then again, she was probably better off not knowing. Hey, what could you say about a woman who was pregnant, and had three possible candidates for the baby's father? Even if all of that *was* a total fabrication? No doubt Riley Hunter considered her to be a woman of remarkably easy virtue.

"Okay," he finally said. "I'll give you a little time. But not one week. Three days. You can have the whole weekend. But come Monday, you'd better make up your mind what you're gonna do. 'Cause before end of business day Monday, one way or another, I'm calling the Wentworths."

Rachel expelled a long sigh of relief. Hey, it was three days more than she'd thought she'd have. And three days could buy Sabrina time enough to get herself thoroughly lost. At this point, she'd take what she could get. "Thank you, Sheriff. You won't be—"

"And in turn," he interrupted her, and suddenly her relief evaporated, "*you* have to give *me*..."

She narrowed her eyes at him. "Yes?"

He smiled that breathtaking rogue's smile again. "Your car keys."

Four

"What?" Rachel said, sure she had misheard.

Sheriff Riley Hunter leaned back in his chair, cupping his head confidently in both hands. "You heard me," he said. "You have to surrender your car keys. I wanna make sure you won't be taking off on me."

"How do you know I won't just rent a car?" But even as she asked the question, Rachel began searching her purse for her key ring.

"We don't have a car rental agency here in Wallace Canyon," he said mildly. "Hell, we only have one gas station. The Chevron right across the street. All I have to do is alert Hal Minger over there to let me know if a beautiful woman with great big, heart-stopping green eyes pulls in for a fill-up, and I'll be on your tail in five minutes flat."

That was a metaphor Rachel would have just as soon done without. It was bad enough that her heart was beating a million miles an hour at the way he had just described her—and with a veritable purr in his voice, too—but then he'd had to go and mention being on her tail, and that had been all it took to fire up some very graphic, very erotic, images in her feverish brain.

She pushed the visions away as best she could and focused on wrestling the key to her five-year-old Saturn off the ring. When it was free, she pushed it reluctantly across the desk toward the sheriff. "How do you know I won't steal a car?" she couldn't resist asking.

His smile grew broader as he covered the key with his hand and squeezed it tight. Something in the gesture set off a little explosion in her midsection, spreading sparks and fire all through her body. She tugged at the turtleneck encircling her throat. Gee, it was getting warm in here all of a sudden. Funny, that.

Sheriff Hunter didn't seem to notice. "You might be a liar, Miss Jensen, but you're no criminal. I can see that now. A mile away."

Yeah, yeah, yeah, she thought. *That's me. Miss Letter of the Law.*

He dropped the key into his shirt pocket and patted it with much satisfaction. "I'll return this to you Monday night."

She bit back a ripe comment, and asked instead, "Just how am I supposed to get around this weekend if I don't have a car?"

"Just how many places do you have to go?" he countered. "You don't seem to have too many ties here. And in case you hadn't noticed, Wallace Canyon's not what you might call a bustling community."

Somehow, she refrained from rolling her eyes. "Oh, believe me, Sheriff. That hasn't escaped my notice."

He crossed his arms over his chest—his incredibly well-formed, truly spectacular, way too sexy chest—and smiled some more. "Well, then," he said.

"Well, then," she agreed. "That still doesn't get me to the few places I'll need to get to. The grocery store, for example. I was planning to pick up a few things on my way back to...on my way home."

He shrugged. "Then call the cops."

A jumpy little flutter of nerves began to whirlpool in her belly at his suggestion. "Anyone in particular I should ask for?"

He nodded.

"Who?"

"Me."

She swallowed hard as the whirlpool of nerves turned into a full-blown twister. "Uh, forgive me, Sheriff, but in spite of Wallace Canyon's peace and quiet, you must have better things to do than chaperon me. I have a little trouble believing that following around a pregnant woman is part of your job description. There are those who might even label something like this harassment."

"Harassment?" he repeated with a chuckle. "You gotta be kidding."

Okay, so she was kidding.

But Sheriff Hunter didn't stop at that. With a suggestive little smile, he added, "Sweetheart, when I want to harass you, you'll know it. Trust me."

Rachel shifted uncomfortably in her chair at the not-so-subtle, sexual overtone of his comment. Well, how did she expect to be treated? she asked herself. A woman who allegedly slept around the way she did and had three fictional candidates for the non-existent paternity of her imaginary child? She'd have to get used to being treated like a trollop.

"I need a ride home," she said succinctly. "With a quick stop at the grocery store."

Sheriff Hunter pushed himself away from his desk and rose to standing, and she tried not to notice how he seemed to flex every muscle as he did so. "Then shall we go?" he asked.

Rachel nodded, resigned to her fate. Whatever. If surrendering her wheels for a weekend, not to mention being thought of as a woman of lax morality, would bring her closer to finding out what was going on with Sabrina, then hoofing it around Wallace Canyon, and fending off Sheriff Hunter's sly little comments, would be a small price to pay. Sabrina's trailer was no more than four or five miles outside of town. If she had to, Rachel could walk that in an hour or so, even if it was way too cold outside for power walking. At least that way, she wouldn't have to rely on Riley Hunter.

She watched in silence as he donned his shearling coat and tucked his hands into his rawhide gloves, then settled his Stetson on his head. Man, he was gorgeous, she noted yet again. He could have been cast in any number of Wild West movies, in any role from cowboy to Comanche, from rustler to ranger. He was just that stunning.

"Miss Jensen?"

When he glanced up, he caught her staring at him, and if she hadn't known better, she would have thought his cheeks stained with the hint of a ruddy blush, something that just about melted her heart. No way did he seem like the kind of man who would blush over something like a woman taking a blatant inventory of his person. Nevertheless, he dropped his gaze back down to his hands and seemed to be inordinately focused on straightening his gloves.

"Yes, Sheriff?" she asked, prodding his question.

He continued to avoid looking at her as he asked, "Which one of the Wentworth boys is most likely to be your baby's father?"

Rachel swallowed hard. For one thing, even if she wasn't Sabrina, the answer to that question was none of his business. For another, although she was indeed vaguely familiar with the Wentworths of Freemont Springs, she hadn't paid such close attention that she remembered any of their names. Nor could she recall now how Sheriff Hunter had identified them earlier in Sabrina's trailer. So, she really had no idea how to answer him.

"Why do you ask?" she said, hedging.

He shrugged, but there was nothing casual about the gesture at all. "Just curious. I know you said it could be either one, but surely one is more likely to be responsible than the other, right? And with Jack dead and all..."

Dead and all? Rachel echoed to herself. Whoa, whoa, whoa. This was the first she'd heard about one of the Wentworths being dead. Unfortunately, there was no way she could ask Sheriff Hunter to elaborate without making herself sound suspicious. If she was that close to the family, she should know one of them had died.

Could that be part of Sabrina's troubles? she wondered. Was that the reason the baby's father wasn't with her? Because he was dead? Oh, poor Sabrina. Suddenly, more than ever before, Rachel wanted to be with her sister. To have been in love like that...to be expecting the baby of a man you loved, only to have lost him...

She had to find Sabrina. She just had to. No way should her twin be alone at a time like this.

"Uhhh..." she murmured, stalling for more time.

Sheriff Hunter glanced up at her again, then immediately dropped his gaze to the floor. "I mean, you didn't...that is, you weren't... It wasn't like you...with both of them, I mean. Well, obviously you did...well, you know...with both of them, if either one could be the father, but...but was one of them...?"

He expelled an exasperated sound, looked up at her again, then immediately right back down at the floor. "Look, forget I said anything, all right? It's none of my business. Just, if you want to talk about it..."

"Um..." she began again.

He was trying so hard to be nice, she thought. Trying so hard to make some sense out of why a woman would end up in the unfortunate—to put it mildly—position that Rachel had lied herself into. The least she could do was try to explain it to him. Try to explain it to herself. To explain it to God, the world and the universe at large.

"Uh, certainly I was more involved with one than the other," she said softly, "but..."

His head snapped up at her offer, his eyes pinning her to the spot, so intense was his unmistakable interest. "Yes?" he said softly.

"Uh..."

"Was it Michael or Jack?" he finally asked.

She expelled a silent sigh of relief at being offered their names flat out that way. "Michael," she said, recalling that Jack was the one he'd listed as dead. "It was Michael. But Jack and I... Well... I guess you could say it was just one of those crazy things, you know?"

He nodded, but still didn't quite seem satisfied by her story. "And this other guy that might be the father? What's the deal with him?"

She sighed, wishing this whole thing would just be over with, so she could stop feeling so guilty—about things she *had* done, and things she hadn't. "Um, he was sort of, uh... That was just one of those crazy things, too," she finally said lamely.

The sheriff nodded, dropping his gaze to the floor. "You like those crazy things, do you?"

Strangely, there was no hint of salaciousness in his voice this time, nothing at all to suggest that he was being, well, suggestive. Nothing to indicate that he intended to take advantage of a woman whose morals were a bit, shall we say, lax. Instead, his question seemed to be generated by a genuine concern for her welfare, by an honest desire to understand just what had happened to her that would cause a woman to wind up in the troubled position that she had put herself in.

Rachel inhaled deeply, wanting very much at that moment to tell him the truth. But at this point, she'd lied so much, had made up so many things, she wondered if Riley Hunter would even believe the truth. And even if he did, she still wasn't quite convinced that she could trust him. So, for now at least, she simply skirted the truth as best she could without quite revealing it.

"No, I don't like those crazy things," she told him. "Just lately... Well, my life's been kind of confusing, and I...I—"

"You're a woman in trouble, huh?" he asked quietly, looking up at her again.

She smiled sadly at the heartfelt concern that darkened his eyes. "Yeah, you could definitely say that," she told him, every bit as quietly.

Although she was grateful to have been able to speak a couple of truths, Rachel knew she had to be careful. If she wasn't, she was going to forget what she'd lied about and what she'd told the truth about, and Riley Hunter would trip her up before her three days came to an end. And until she was absolutely positive that she could trust him with Sabrina's safety, she just wasn't willing to reveal all the facts.

Best just to avoid him after today, she thought. She could hole up in Sabrina's trailer for the weekend, call some friends and acquaintances, make her plans from there. Then... Well, somehow, she was just going to have to track down her sister. That was all there was to it.

"After you, Miss Jensen," Riley Hunter said, interrupting her thoughts.

Rachel was about to say something more, then decided she'd

been skirting the edge of the truth—and her sanity—long enough now, thank you very much, and there was no reason to borrow more trouble than she already had. So she only smiled weakly and dipped her head in silent acknowledgment. Then, before Sheriff Hunter had a chance to ask her anything else that might immerse her even deeper, Rachel snapped up her coat and preceded him out of his office.

And she hoped like crazy that three days would be enough for her to make sense of this whole crazy thing.

Riley was folding himself back into his sheriff's utility vehicle—having responded to the latest complaint about the notorious howling Barker family—when visions of Sabrina Jensen started dancing around in his head like a mess of sugar plum fairies. Then again, he hadn't been able to think about much of anything *but* Sabrina Jensen since meeting her yesterday afternoon, so that wasn't exactly surprising, was it?

Still, it rankled to realize that she commanded so much of his preoccupation time—time he could have been spending on far more important pursuits—when he hadn't even enjoyed more than a few hours in her company. He'd never had a woman get under his skin so quickly, so completely, and the knowledge that one like Sabrina had managed to wheedle her way in just didn't set well with him at all.

A man liked to think that when he was attracted solely to one woman—especially with the intensity that Riley found himself wanting Sabrina—then that woman was solely attracted to him, too. But Sabrina... Well, hell. There was a woman who didn't even know which of three men had fathered her baby. Three men. *Three men.* Not that Riley was one to pass judgment on another person's life-style—hey, live and let live was his one true motto—but, daggone it: Why did he have to fall so hard for a woman like that?

Then again, he reminded himself, the last woman he'd fallen hard and fast for had been a pillar of the community, hadn't she? Miss Caroline Merilee Dewhurst had been a regular church-goer, a former Girl Scout, a Junior Leaguer, a prim little first-grade teacher, *and* a virgin. And look how *that* had turned out. The minute her folks had threatened to pull the plug on her allowance and her trust fund if she married some common riffraff like Riley Hunter, she'd run right back to their loving arms and married the man they chose for her.

So much for love and devotion.

Maybe Riley was just destined to fall in love with women who didn't fall in love back with him. No doubt there was a twelve-step program somewhere for guys like him. He ought to go out and look for one of those self-help books: *Women Who Have Three Possible Candidates for Father of Their Baby, and the Men Who Love Them—and Aren't, by the Way, the Father of Their Baby.*

He turned the key in the ignition and stared out the windshield at the dark sky overhead. He saw a full moon hanging bright as a silver dollar above him, a scattering of stars playing hide-and-seek with a handful of clouds, and a pair of haunting green eyes, full of fear and worry, gazing back at him.

He'd always been a sucker for women in trouble, he recalled, starting way back in second grade, when he'd seen Sarah Sandusky being picked on by some of the bigger girls at school. They'd been making fun of her because her family was poor and her father had skipped out on them. Riley had taken Sarah under his wing that very morning, had made sure no one ever said an ill word toward her again. And the two of them had remained friends to this day. Now she was happily married, worked as a features reporter for the Tulsa newspaper, and had a pretty dag-gone good life. She and her husband had even asked Riley to be godfather to their firstborn son.

Who was to say that Sabrina Jensen hadn't been treated the same way as Sarah at some point in her life? Maybe she'd been picked on, too, when she was a kid. Maybe she'd been poor. Maybe she'd been abandoned. And maybe there had never been anybody to step in and defend her or offer her a shoulder for support. Riley had long been a believer that the only thing separating the winners and losers in life was that the winners had good friends and a loving family to support them through the rough times, and the losers had nobody.

Sabrina Jensen sure didn't seem to have anybody. Hadn't she

hinted as much yesterday, when he'd suggested that it was suspicious to want to get away during the holidays, when most folks wanted to be with their loved ones? What was it she had said? That it depended on one's relationship with one's loved ones. Evidently, the Jensen family ties were none too tight.

And now here she was, miles from home, living in a rented trailer, with no one to check on her to see if she was doing okay. With no one to even wonder or care about her, except a family who wasn't even hers, but thought she might be carrying a child that belonged to one of their own. Sabrina Jensen was probably scared, uncertain and worried, not just about herself, but about her unborn child, too. Yet she had no one—no one—to turn to for help.

And here it was almost Christmas, too.

Riley flicked on the headlights and threw the truck into gear. The Westport Trailer Park, or Mobile Home Community, or whatever the hell it wanted to call itself these days, wasn't but a couple of miles away from where he was right now—namely, the notorious howling Barker family's compound. It wouldn't take but a minute to swing by there and make sure Sabrina was okay. Billy Barker was still unaccounted for, and was doubtless out there roaming the landscape. Not that he was capable of any major mischief. Well, besides howling, anyway. But Sabrina might not realize that, should she hear him wailing off in the distance. Even if they were harmless, the notorious howling Barker family could be powerful spooky when they set their minds to it.

Yeah, Riley thought, maybe he should just run by Sabrina's place real quick and make sure she was okay. See if she needed anything. Or anyone.

The lights were still on in her trailer when he rolled to a stop out front. Not that that was such a startling discovery, seeing as how it was barely nine-thirty. Even at that, Riley hesitated before getting out of the truck. He didn't kid himself that his intentions were entirely honorable. Yeah, he wanted to make sure she was okay and everything, but he'd be lying if he didn't admit that a part of him was drawn to Sabrina for considerably more...well, *earthy*...reasons. He reminded himself that earthy reasons had gotten him into trouble before. Did he really need that again?

Brushing the thoughts aside, he opened the door and got out of the truck. Sabrina must have heard him pull up, because before he even made it to the bottom step of her trailer, he glanced up to find her standing framed by the open door, a faint yellow light from within spilling out around her.

She was dressed in what probably passed for her pajamas, a big ol' red flannel shirt that hung down to her knees over white thermal leggings, a pair of heavy socks hugging her feet and ankles. She'd pulled her hair back in a ponytail that rode high on her head, but a handful of the silky dark tresses in front fell haphazardly around a face scrubbed clean of what little makeup she had worn that afternoon. Her right hand clutched the front door as if she were clinging to it for some kind of life support, and in her left hand she held—

Hold on there. Riley narrowed his eyes suspiciously. She was holding a glass of white wine. Mighty odd beverage for a pregnant woman to be enjoying. Even if Sabrina *had* professed to not being an expert when it came to having a baby, it didn't take a genius to remember that pregnant women weren't supposed to consume anything alcoholic.

"Miss Jensen," he said, lifting two fingers to the brim of his Stetson in greeting.

"Sheriff," she replied in a cautious voice. "What brings you out this way this time of night?"

He took a few steps forward, until he stood at the bottom of the metal stairs leading up to her front door. "I was out on a call concerning the notorious howling Barker family. Thought I'd stop by to see how you were doing."

She eyed him curiously. "A call concerning who?"

"The notorious howling Barker family," he repeated. "They're sort of a local legend around here. There's a whole mess of them, and they don't live but a few miles away from here."

"Are they dangerous?"

"No, ma'am," he hastened to assure her. "Just annoying as hell."

"Oh."

"Anyway, the youngest, Billy Barker, he's still out and about. He wouldn't hurt a fly, but, like I said, he can be pretty annoying. I just wanted to make sure he left you alone. You being a newcomer to the community and all, he might see you as fair game."

Her eyebrows knitted downward in clear concern. "Just what does a, um, a notorious howling Barker do?"

Riley settled a hand on the flimsy stair rail, then glanced down at the ground as he stubbed the toe of his cowboy boot in the dust. "Mostly, they just, well, you know…howl at stuff. The moon. Passing cars. Neighbors' dogs. Everly Brothers music. That kind of thing. Pretty much whatever takes their fancy."

"I see."

He glanced up at the inky night sky. "The moon's the worst, though. When it's full like this, they can get pretty loud. I'm surprised you didn't hear anything."

She pointed toward the interior of the trailer with her free hand. "I've had the radio on kind of loud." She smiled a little tremulously. "I'm surprised you didn't get any complaints about me."

For the first time, Riley noted the not-so-faint strains of a country-and-western version of "I Saw Mommy Kissing Santa Claus." He nodded. "That's nothing compared to the notorious howling Barkers."

She replaced her hand on the door, as if she were preparing to shut it. "Well, as you can see, I'm perfectly fine. Thanks for the concern, Sheriff, but if there's nothing else…?"

Unable to help himself, Riley said, "Actually, there is one thing."

She halted the motion of closing the door and met his gaze levelly. "Yes?"

He dipped his head toward the wineglass in her hand. "Are you sure it's a good idea to be drinking wine in your condition? No offense, ma'am, but that just doesn't seem healthy for the little nipper inside you."

Sabrina's eyes widened at his remark, and he wondered if he'd overstepped his bounds. It really wasn't any of his business, Riley told himself. She wasn't his responsibility, and neither was her baby. But he couldn't have slept tonight if he hadn't done something to draw her attention to the fact that what she was doing might be potentially harmful to her unborn child. Hell, for all he knew, maybe she *didn't* know she wasn't supposed to be drinking.

"Uhhh..." she responded, stretching the single syllable out over several zip codes. Then, finally, her vocabulary seemed to kick back in. "Not to worry," she said, her words quick and clipped. "It's some of that nonalcoholic wine they make now. Honest."

Riley expelled a mental sigh of relief. Of course. He'd forgotten they made that stuff.

"I just always feel so festive this time of year," she continued before he had a chance to comment, the dubious cheer in her voice sounding forced, strained. "I like to stock up on all that holiday fare. If you'll recall, I even bought a cheese ball at the grocery store yesterday. Gotta have a cheese ball at Christmastime, you know, or else it wouldn't be...um...Christmastime."

"Yes, ma'am, I do recall that particular purchase. You seemed to be pretty excited about it at the time."

And she had been, Riley remembered. When she'd stumbled on that refrigerated bin full of port wine cheese balls, she'd been like a kid in a candy store. Kept murmuring stuff about how it wouldn't be Christmas without cheese balls. At the time, he'd thought she was overreacting a bit, but evidently, this was a vital part of her holiday celebration.

"And I can't possibly enjoy a cheese ball without a glass of wine," she continued. "So I dug out a bottle of this fake chardonnay that I brought with me from Oklahoma City." As if to illustrate just how much she was enjoying herself, she took a generous sip and murmured, "Mmm. It's so good. I'd invite you in for a glass, but I'm sure you have other places to be, so..."

Had it been real wine, Riley would have declined in a heartbeat. Where he could drink any man in Oklahoma under the table when it came to Bourbon or Scotch or some such thing—not that he did much drinking, but he could if he wanted to—wine went straight to his head. He couldn't have more than one glass without landing flat on his back and waking up with one doozy of a hangover the following morning. But since this obviously wasn't real wine, and since it was the delectable Sabrina Jensen offering...

"On the contrary," he said. "I'm actually off the clock right now. So I wouldn't mind joining you for a glass at all. Thanks for the invite."

Her eyes widened in what he could only liken to panic at his agreement. "You wouldn't?" she said.

"Don't you want me to?" he asked, his suspicion rousing all over again.

"No, it's not that, just..."

"What?"

"Well, I'm just surprised, is all. That you're not working, I mean. Especially since you said you were just finishing up a call."

Riley gripped the stair rail more tightly and pulled himself slowly up the stairs until he reached the last one, which, even standing a step below her, brought him a little taller than face-to-face with Sabrina Jensen.

"Even if I'm not always on the clock, I'm always working," he told her. "In a little town like Wallace Canyon, I'm perpetually on call. Fortunately, in a little town like Wallace Canyon, nothing much happens to make me lose any sleep. So, yeah, I guess, technically, you could say I'm working. But you could also say I'm giving myself the rest of the night off. Now, about that glass of fake chardonnay?" he asked before she could rescind her offer. For some reason, he suddenly wanted very badly to spend a little more time with Sabrina Jensen.

"Uh..." she said again.

For a moment, she only pinned him in place with her gaze, the sight of her green eyes warming him right up, in spite of their coolness. Then, finally, she stepped away from the door and thrust her arm inside, beckoning him to enter.

"Sure," she said halfheartedly. "Sure, there's plenty. I hope you like cheese balls, too."

"Wouldn't be Christmas without 'em," he echoed her earlier sentiment.

The moment he closed the door behind himself, Sabrina quickly turned down the radio and dashed to the kitchen, and

Riley went about discarding his hat and gloves and coat. Because he'd been at home when the call had come about the notorious howling Barker family, he wasn't wearing his uniform. Instead, he'd donned a pair of well-worn blue jeans and an even better worn denim work shirt. As was his habit, the moment his hat was off his head, he ran the fingers of both hands through his hair to smooth out the razor-straight, coal black tresses. He didn't pay attention to Sabrina's movements about the kitchen this time, re-calling all too well what had happened the last time he'd done that. So by the time he'd made himself comfortable on the settee, she was returning with a glass of wine for him that was identical to her own.

"Here you go," she said. "Hope you like it."

Riley sipped, and found the flavor to be very good. He'd al-ways suspected those nonalcoholic versions of alcohol probably tasted worse than horse doody, but this was surprisingly good. "I like it," he said before enjoying another healthy sip. To be polite, he added, "I might have to get some of this for myself. What kind is it?"

Again, there was a faint widening of Sabrina Jensen's eyes before she answered. "Uh...it's um... I think it's called *Château de l'Imposteur.*"

Riley nodded slowly. "It's right tasty."

She nodded quickly in return. "Um, yeah," she agreed. "It's especially good with chicken and fish."

"I'll remember that."

For an awkward moment, neither of them said a word. Then Sabrina moved quickly to the chair she had occupied the day before and inhaled a big sip of her fake wine. "So, Sheriff," she began.

He held up a hand to stop her. "Please. You might as well call me Riley. Just about everyone else in Wallace Canyon does. Even the people I arrest."

"You've actually arrested people here?" she asked with a smile. "I find that hard to believe."

He smiled back. "Yeah, well it's a necessary part of the job every now and then."

"The notorious howling Barkers?" she guessed.

He nodded. "And the less notorious Glendenning sisters."

"What have they done?"

Riley chuckled. "Halloween pranks, mostly. Toilet paper in the trees, soaping windows, shooting off shotguns in the middle of the night, that kind of thing. Except that they like to do that stuff year-round, and sometimes they go a bit too far." He sipped his wine again before adding, "Hell, they're both in their eighties. You'd think they'd've outgrown it by now."

She laughed softly and studied him in silence for a moment. "Forgive me, Sheriff...I mean, Riley," she corrected herself when he opened his mouth to do it for her. "And you might as well call me, uh...Sabrina," she said before continuing. "But Wallace Canyon seems like an unlikely spot for someone like you to be working. Don't get me wrong," she quickly qualified. "You have a nice little community here, but it doesn't seem to require the services of someone as...as capable as you obviously are."

"You asking me what's brought me to this uncharted, desolate corner of the state, Miss... I mean...Sabrina?" he likewise corrected himself, liking the way her name felt on his tongue. He wondered if the rest of her would respond as nicely to his mouth. Then, immediately, he pushed the thought away. No sense wandering down a road that led to nowhere, he thought.

She shrugged. "I told you my story. Turnabout's fair play."

He supposed she was right, but Riley didn't much like being on the receiving end of an interrogation. Especially when it involved himself and his own past. Still, it wasn't as if he had anything to hide.

So he shrugged and began, "I'm originally from a little town not too far outside Tulsa. I grew up in Edenside. If you've got ties to Tulsa, then maybe you've heard of it?"

She nodded, keeping her features carefully schooled into a blank expression, which was what any polite person would do when they encountered somebody who was a product of Edenside. "I know where it is," she said, dropping her gaze down to her glass. "Can't say as I get down that way much myself, though, when I visit with...Aunt Wisteria."

"Not too many people do," he agreed with a chuckle that was totally lacking in good humor. "Nothing there but a bunch of run-down old shotgun houses and a county dump site. Oh, yeah, and I almost forgot—rampant crime. In spite of its name, Edenside's not the kind of place most people want to find themselves. Especially after dark."

She offered no comment to that, only sipped her wine again before asking, "So, what got you out of Edenside?"

It was a subject that Riley normally would have just as soon not talked about, but for some reason, discussing his past with Sabrina didn't feel as awkward as it always had with other people. Maybe because he suspected that the two of them probably had something in common in that respect.

"My daddy took off when I was seven and my sister was five," he said, "leaving my mom with two kids and three jobs to bring us up. Mama was the kind of woman who wanted to make sure her kids got a better life than she had. She made sure we both went to college. And we did."

"What did you study?" Sabrina asked.

"Justice administration," he replied proudly. "Got my BS with honors. Before coming out this way, I worked as a homicide detective for the Tulsa PD."

"No kidding? That's very interesting," she said, her expression lightening up, as if she found this information about him to be *very* interesting indeed. She brought her knees up before her, then moved them to the side and tucked her feet underneath her, assuming a pose that, for all its innocence, Riley found very provocative for some reason.

So, he glanced back down at his fake wine and enjoyed another hefty sip. Boy, it really was good. There was no way he would have guessed this wasn't the real thing. After he swallowed, he continued, "I spent almost ten years on the Tulsa police force. Started off in uniform when I was twenty-two and worked my way up."

"Why did you leave?"

He sighed heavily, enjoyed another lengthy sip of his wine and avoided her gaze. "I just didn't have a thick enough hide to work homicide," he told her frankly. Hell, it didn't bother Riley to admit such a thing. It definitely took a stronger person than he was to be able to work a job like that, day in and day out, and not go crazy. "I quit not long after wrapping up a case that involved a man who murdered his six-year-old son," he added bluntly.

Sabrina's lips parted in dismay, and she lifted a hand to cover them, but she said nothing in response to his assertion.

"After that," he said, "I just couldn't do it anymore. I couldn't stand seeing what other people were capable of doing to each other. When I saw an ad for this position in the paper, I suddenly had this real intense desire to get away from the city, so I jumped on the opportunity. So far, working here in Wallace Canyon has suited my needs just fine."

Of course, there was another reason Riley had exiled himself to the corner of the world this way. He'd needed the time a job like this one could afford him to work on what he'd always thought of as his avocation, an avocation he was hoping to make a vocation one of these days. And being sheriff of Wallace Canyon suited his needs in that department, too. In fact, moving out here had been just about the smartest thing Riley had ever done, had brought him a peace of mind and a tranquillity of spirit unlike any he'd ever experienced.

Until yesterday, anyway. Sabrina Jensen's arrival in Wallace Canyon had gone a long way to disrupt his peace and tranquillity. A long, *long* way. And somehow, as he sipped his phony wine and watched her over the rim of the glass, he suspected he wasn't anywhere near his final destination on that one.

Five

"So, what do you do back in Oklahoma City?"

Rachel studied Riley Hunter in the pale light of the single lamp glowing beside her and really wished she hadn't invited him inside. Of course, when she'd done that, she hadn't for a moment thought he would actually take her up on the invitation. She'd figured he was working, or that he'd been on his way somewhere else, and that he was just being polite in stopping by to check on her. The last thing she'd expected was that he'd want to be anywhere closer to her than he absolutely had to be. The way he'd been acting yesterday, she'd thought he'd be glad to be rid of her.

Although, now that she thought back on it, he had been awfully nice to her at the little market where they'd stopped to pick up a few groceries before returning to Sabrina's trailer. He'd carried the little basket for her, had reached up to all the high shelves she couldn't make herself, had reminded her to buy a lot of the things that a pregnant woman would need in addition to Rachel's usual diet of Cheetos and Cherry Coke. It had been Riley who'd tossed the oatmeal and orange juice, the lean meat and skim milk, and—against her objections—the broccoli and brussels sprouts, into the grocery basket.

And it was Riley who had reminded her that a pregnant woman shouldn't be drinking wine, she recalled now, battling back a blush. Which, of course, Rachel should have remembered when she went to meet him at the front door. She just hadn't been thinking. As usual.

At the last minute, before leaving Oklahoma City, she'd grabbed a bottle of chardonnay from the little wine rack atop her fridge and packed it in her bag. At the time, she'd suspected her stay with Sabrina was going to be a lengthy one, and she frequently liked to have a glass of wine at night while reading, before going to bed. But in her flustered state at seeing Riley again, she'd forgotten all about the fact that she was supposed to be posing as a pregnant woman. And when he'd called her on her transgression of imbibing, she'd been forced to lie to him.

Again.

Would there ever come a time, she wondered, when she would be able to say something to him that *wasn't* a lie? Then she recalled that he had just asked her what she did in Oklahoma City. Well, here was her chance, she thought. If he didn't know Sabrina was seven months pregnant, then chances were he didn't know anything about her sister's life-style. So, what the heck, Rachel thought. She could at least be honest with him about her life back home.

"I tend bar," she said. "At least, I *used to* tend bar. I sort of lost my job just before I left."

"You got fired at Christmastime?" he asked. "That's terrible. Especially with you being pregnant and all."

She nibbled her lip fretfully. "Yeah, well, um…my boss didn't know I was pregnant."

"You should have told him."

"I don't think it would have made a difference." That, too, was the truth, she thought. Eddie, her bar manager, had a heart of ice. Or, at least, he would have had a heart of ice. If he'd had a heart at all. That jerk.

"Maybe I could call him and talk to him," Riley offered. "Remind him about humanity and charity and how important it is this time of year.''

"No!" Rachel said too quickly, too adamantly. She realized how overzealous she'd been when Riley snapped his head back to look at her. "I mean," she tried again, "it's none of his business. I don't want him to know about my...my condition. Don't worry about me. I'll find another job. There's always somebody hiring bartenders. Don't give it a second thought."

Judging by the look on his face, Riley would doubtless be giving it a lot more than a second thought, Rachel noted. He really did seem worried about her, she marveled. He honestly appeared to be concerned that she wasn't going to be able to take care of herself and her unborn baby.

Boy, she must be a better liar than she thought she was.

The realization twisted something painfully inside Rachel, and she found herself again wanting to tell him the truth. He was really much too sweet a person to be duped this way. Nevertheless, she needn't be hasty. There would be time enough later to be honest with him. Once she knew for sure that Sabrina was safe.

"You're a good guy, Riley," she said with a smile, satisfying her honest tendencies with that remark. "But really, you don't have to worry about me."

His cheeks stained with that ruddy blush again, and he hastily dropped his gaze down into his wineglass. "I'm not that good a guy," he said softly. "I just hate to see a woman like you in trouble, that's all."

"I can take care of myself," she told him, retreating to half-truths again.

He expelled a dubious sound and glanced up at her again. "Yeah, well, that's probably open to debate, isn't it?"

Rachel bristled. "It's none of your business," she reminded him.

"I know," he said softly. He inhaled another generous mouthful of his wine, his eyes never leaving hers. After he swallowed, he added, "But that doesn't keep me from caring about what happens to you."

This time, something inside Rachel began to grow warm at the sound of his quietly uttered statement. He'd barely known her a day, and he cared about what happened to her. As far as he was concerned, she was a woman who currently had more trouble in her life than she could shake a stick at, and he cared about her. She'd lied her way into a position that would have most men running, screaming in terror, in the opposite direction, but he cared about her.

This was just what she needed, Rachel thought morosely. Because way down deep inside herself, she cared about Riley, too. Even after knowing him such a short time. Even with the knowledge that when it came to caring for men, she was way too susceptible.

Even if there was something...different...about her reaction this time.

That was ridiculous, Rachel told herself. What could be any different about the feelings she had for Riley Hunter than she'd had for any other man in her life? Usually, when Rachel fell for a guy, it was with all her heart, all her soul and all her might. And scarcely a week went by that she *didn't* meet a man she fell for. Working as a bartender meant she met *a lot* of men, every single day of her life. Men who flirted with her and teased her, men who, without even trying, could cause her to fall head over heels in love with them before the night was through. And Rachel had learned a *looong* time ago to be very, very careful about who she gave her heart to.

So she gave it to no one. Oh, sure, she flirted and teased right back, and her heart broke a little bit every night when she went home alone to an empty apartment. But if a guy asked her to go out, she flatly turned him down, no questions asked or answered. She'd made a mistake with a man once, when she was seventeen, and she wasn't going to let it happen again.

She'd fallen for a truly charming cowboy named Bart Mendoza within hours of meeting him, and before the week was out, she'd completely surrendered herself to him, mind, body and soul. But before another week was out, he'd up and left without even saying goodbye. Shortly after that, Rachel had forgotten all about him, because she'd met a charmer named Nathan who had put thoughts of Bart right out of her head. And shortly after that, she'd met another charmer named Tim, who had made her forget all about Nathan.

Not that she'd gone so far as to give herself to Nathan or Tim the way she had Bart. Nor had she allowed herself to go too far with any of the others who came after them, no sir. Rachel's experience with Bart had been painful, but worthwhile, one that had taught her a lesson, but good. Because it had shown her once and for all that she was exactly the same kind of woman as her mother—her head was turned by the first handsome face that came along, just as her mother's had been.

Rachel didn't remember her mama well, not having seen her since she was a toddler, but she knew Blanche Jensen had abandoned her twin daughters and a loving husband because a good-looking, sweet-talking man had charmed his way into her life and led her away.

Oh, sure, there had been the sporadic birthday card or letter from time to time when the girls were still little, but gradually, even those had ceased. Blanche made her choice the day she left them, and she'd never looked back. She'd been swayed by a handsome face, charmed by a simple flirtation, enough that she washed her hands of her own family.

Bart Mendoza had charmed his way into Rachel's life. And so had scores of other men in the years that had passed since then. But unlike with Bart, she hadn't let herself be swayed so completely by those other men. She'd let herself fall in love with them for the few hours she spent with them, and once they were gone, she'd put them firmly out of mind. She might have done some stupid things in her life—and she would doubtless do a lot more before her time on earth was over—but Rachel wasn't going to repeat that particular mistake twice.

She was *not* going to be the kind of woman her mother was, moving from one lover to the next—heck, one *husband* to the next—with no more concern for any of them than she had for a run in her panty hose. And if that meant Rachel had to be alone for the rest of her life, well, then...so be it. There were certainly worse things that could happen to a person than solitude.

So she wasn't going to be swayed by Riley Hunter, she vowed on the spot. Because she knew if she let herself fall for him, she'd do something she'd soon regret. As sweet and as nice as he was, Riley Hunter, she was certain, was just like every other handsome, charming man in the world. Rachel would fall in love with him in two seconds flat—heck, she'd already fallen for him in less than two seconds flat—and the minute he was out of her life, she'd fall right back out of love.

So as much as she liked Riley, there was absolutely no point in pursuing whatever strange, warm, fuzzy sensations he was making her feel. Which, now that she thought about it, was maybe another good reason for lying to him about her real identity. In addition to protecting Sabrina, she was protecting herself.

"I appreciate you caring about what happens to me," she said in response to his concern. "But whether you believe me or not, I can take care of myself."

"Fine," he said softly, draining the rest of his wine. "If you insist, I guess I have no choice but to believe you."

No choice but to believe her, Rachel echoed to herself. That was a good one.

"Well," he began again, looking around for a place to set his empty glass, "I don't guess there's much point in me hanging around, now that I see how capable you are of taking care of yourself."

Having found no resting place for his glass, he rose quickly from the settee, presumably to head for the kitchen. But the action must have been too fast for his equilibrium, because instead of taking a step forward, he only stood still, wavering a bit, his eyes widening in obvious surprise. Then, before Rachel realized what was happening, he went careening forward, right toward her. Abruptly, she stood, too, but only wound up trying to catch him— with little success—as he lurched forward.

"Whoa," he said as he cupped his hands over her shoulders to keep himself from falling face first into her...well, into her chest. But the motion of his body was much too powerful for her to have any effect on halting it, and in spite of her efforts, the two of them fell backward, Rachel into the chair she had just vacated, and Riley into her lap.

For one split second, they sat staring at each other, as if neither could figure out what on earth had just happened. Then Riley leapt up again, his eyes wide with fear, murmuring something about not wanting to hurt the baby. But his retreat only landed him back on the settee, this time sprawled in a *much* less formal position than the one he had been enjoying before, arms thrown out to his sides, legs spread wide, one booted foot on the floor, the other dangling over the side.

Rachel didn't—couldn't—move from the chair, only sat there blinking at him, as if a too bright flash had just gone off right in front of her eyes. Then, gradually, she took stock of their positions. And, too late, she realized that Riley's, at least, was in no way appropriate for a man of the law.

"Wh-what happened?" she stammered.

He shook his head hard, as if to clear it, then pressed both hands to his forehead. "What the hell...?" he said, his words fading before he completed the thought.

"What?" Rachel asked again. "What's wrong?"

"If I didn't know better," Riley said softly, his hands still cupped over his forehead, his gaze faintly accusing, "I'd swear I was drunk."

A little explosion went off in Rachel's midsection, and she scrambled for another lie. "What?" she said. "That's impossible."

And it should have been, she told herself. She'd only filled his glass half-full. Heck, she'd had more to drink than Riley had, and she didn't even feel a faint buzz. He was a big man who had just consumed one little, itty-bitty glass of wine. Even if she had lied about it being nonalcoholic, Riley Hunter was *not* the kind of man to get tipsy over something like that. At least, he didn't *seem* to be.

"You sure that stuff wasn't the real thing?" he asked.

"Positive," she lied.

"Because I have a real low tolerance for wine," he added.

Oh, fine, Rachel thought. *Now* he told her. Aloud, though, all she said was, "Oh?"

"Oh, yeah."

"Gee."

At her lack of reaction, he shook his head again. "And I haven't felt this woozy since my sister's wedding reception, when one glass of champagne floored me. Literally. I just can't handle wine at all.''

"Oh?" she said again, this time in a very small voice.

Riley eyed her thoughtfully for a moment before continuing. And when he did, it was to say, much to her relief, "Come to think of it, though, I sorta felt this way when I had the flu last winter. But I sure don't get sick very often. Especially not like this.''

Rachel seized that comment for all it was worth. "You know, there has been something going around," she said quickly. "Hits real hard, real fast. Maybe that's what you've got. A nasty flu bug." She jumped up from her chair and raced for the bathroom. "You better let me take your temperature.''

"No," he called out from behind her. "I don't think that'll be necessary. I don't feel warm at all.''

He didn't feel warm? Rachel marveled, stung. After that little impromptu tango they'd just done where he'd ended up in her lap? Here she had a raging inferno eating up her insides, and he wasn't even *warm?* Well, wasn't *that* just a fine howdy-do?

"Okay," she muttered, abandoning the bathroom before entering and returning to her chair. She perched herself on the very edge and watched Riley warily. He had straightened himself up some, but was leaning forward now with his elbows propped on his knees, his head cradled carefully in his hands.

"I'm telling you, I feel drunk," he said again without looking up.

From one glass of wine? Rachel thought. Just what kind of stuff were cowboy sheriffs made of nowadays? "Maybe it was vertigo," she suggested.

He shook his head—slowly, she noted—then groaned a bit. "I don't suffer from vertigo.''

"Maybe it was one of those temporary vertigo things.''

That, at last, made him look up. But he didn't seem to feel too good. "Temporary vertigo?" he echoed doubtfully.

She nodded quickly.

"Never heard of it.''

"My aunt Wisteria suffers from it," she said. "Maybe if you just sit quietly for a minute you'll feel better.''

"I think I'd rather lie down."

Oh, no, no, no, no, no, Rachel thought. *I don't think so.* The last thing she needed was a gorgeous sheriff passed out on her sister's rented couch. But before she could say a word to object, Riley Hunter turned and lay flat on the settee, one arm bent over his eyes. Rachel opened her mouth to say something, had no idea what, then snapped it shut again. And within two minutes, Riley Hunter was sound asleep.

"Unbelievable," she muttered. This time she was the one to shake her head.

She glanced at the clock in the kitchen. Not even 10:00 p.m. and Riley was down for the count. She sighed heavily. Now what? She had planned to make a few more phone calls tonight, but it looked as though that wouldn't be happening now. Not when she had a man of the law snoozing right next to the telephone. Nope, not much left for her to do but tidy up, throw a blanket over her law enforcement officer and head to bed herself. Good thing she'd brought a book to read, she thought. 'Cause there wasn't much else for her to do tonight.

Pitiful, Rachel, she chastised herself fifteen minutes later as she snuggled down under the covers on the allegedly full-size bed in Sabrina's rented bedroom. Here she was, sharing quarters with a hunka hunka burnin' love like Riley Hunter, and he was snoring to wake the devil. Not that she would have succumbed to any kind of hanky-panky or anything like that, but it sure didn't help a woman's self-esteem to realize that a sexy man who thought she'd done some serious sleeping around in her time wasn't even interested enough to try and take advantage of her.

Opening her book to where she'd left off that afternoon, Rachel pushed the thought away and tried to ignore Riley's snoring not fifteen feet away. It was going to be a long night.

Riley awoke slowly and in quite severe pain. There was a crick in his neck, a charley horse in his leg, a stitch in his side, and a throbbing pain in his head. And all he could do for the first few minutes was lie motionless with his eyes shut tight, wondering where in the hell he was and who in the hell had beat him up so bad to make him feel like this. Man, he hadn't done anything to anybody that would warrant this kind of thumping. Not lately, anyway.

Gradually, the aroma of brewing coffee registered in his feeble brain, as did the crackle of bacon frying, the scratchy feel of a blanket under his chin, and the soft murmur of a woman humming "Frosty the Snowman" under her breath. Only the allure of such messages to his senses made him risk opening one eye.

Immediately, however, he was forced to shut it again, because the faint light of early dawn just about sliced his forehead in two. Inhaling a deep breath, Riley tried again—more slowly this time—and met with a bit of success. Okay. One eye open. Surely he could get the other one to at least half-mast. With no small effort, and after several tries, he did just that. Hot dog. He was movin' right along now.

But having his eyes open—well, sorta open, anyway—helped him assess his situation not at all. Above him was a cheap-looking ceiling that played host to a big water stain, and beneath him was a lumpy—and way too short—mattress. His apartment above the police station wasn't exactly the Holiday Inn by any stretch of the imagination, but even he had a few more creature comforts than this place boasted. Just where in the hell was he, and who in the hell—

"Oh, you're awake."

A woman's voice. Now that *really* threw him, because he hadn't been anywhere near a woman in any romantic sense since coming to Wallace Canyon. Certainly there was no way he could have wound up in one's bed. So, who could possibly be the owner of that sweet, warm, delicious-sounding—

Sabrina Jensen.

Like a ton of fake wine, it hit him, and in a rush of recollection, he remembered his activities of the night before. He'd been checking up on a beautiful pregnant woman who was totally clueless as to the paternity of her baby—among other things—and she'd invited him in for a glass of phony chardonnay. They'd exchanged a few heated words and few more—even hotter—glances, and then... Well, then he'd passed out drunk. At least, he sure had felt drunk. That *Château de l'Imposteur* stuff had gone straight to his head.

Vaguely, from the darkened, cobwebbed corners of his mind, he remembered reading somewhere that even the nonalcoholic versions of beer and wine still had some negligible amounts of alcohol in them. Not enough to be considered dangerous—at least, not to most people—but evidently even a trace amount could topple a man like him. Man, he must have some kind of allergy or something for that stuff to have hit him so hard.

Or else Sabrina Jensen had been lying to him. Again.

Somehow, he managed to lever himself up off the settee, noting absently the blanket that fell to the floor when he did. Beneath it, his clothing was a little wrinkled and stale smelling, but none the worse for wear, and his boots still hugged his feet. Slowly—whoa, *very* slowly—he ran his fingers through his hair, then scrubbed both hands vigorously over his smooth face. Thanks to the purity of his Cherokee heritage, he didn't have to worry much about shaving—he had no facial hair to speak of, nor any on his chest, either. His teeth and tongue, however, suddenly felt as if they needed a haircut real bad.

He was about to open his mouth to put voice to one of the many questions circling in his brain, when a cup of coffee appeared beneath his nose, and its strong aroma distracted him.

"Decaf," Sabrina told him, her voice a scarce whisper, for which he was profoundly grateful. "But maybe if we don't talk about it too loudly, we can fool your brain into thinking that it's the real thing."

He glanced up at her as he took the cup from her hand, and she lifted a finger to her lips and smiled at him, as if the two of them shared a small secret. She looked as good as he felt bad, and he shook his head morosely—*very* slowly again—before sipping carefully of the dark brew. Even if it didn't have the heavy dose of caffeine his body was clamoring for right now, just the flavor and warmth went a long way toward making him feel better.

The sight of Sabrina went even further, though. Her dark brown hair fell loose around her face again, those green eyes fairly sparkling, even in the scant light of the trailer. She, too, had her fingers wrapped around a mug of coffee, which she lifted to her mouth for an idle sip. A baggy, bright red sweatshirt tumbled down over her jeans-clad hips, and heavy hiking boots warmed her feet. Again, Riley found his gaze falling to her belly, and again, he wondered about the life growing inside her, and the man who was partly responsible for it.

"How you feeling?" he asked her, focusing his attention back on the coffee he shifted from one hand to the other, trying to ignore the aches and pains that each little movement roused in his body.

"I should be asking you the same question," she said.

"I asked you first."

She chuckled softly. "I feel fine. Never better. You?"

He sipped his coffee slowly, carefully, before replying, "Ask me again in about an hour."

She smiled. "Okay, I will. Bacon and eggs all right for breakfast?"

He managed a nod. "Fine. You don't have any of that morning sickness?" he asked, glancing up at her again.

For just a fraction of a second, Riley was once more overcome by the sensation that she was hiding something. Then she shook her head quickly, and the feeling was gone.

"No," she told him. "As I said, I've never felt better. Just, um, a lot hungrier than usual."

As if prodded by her statement, and in spite of the hangover rocking him, his stomach growled in protest to its empty state. He hadn't eaten any supper last night, he remembered, because the call about the notorious howling Barker family had come right when he was trying to decide which of the boxed-and-bagged delicacies in the freezer to nuke in the microwave. In fact, now that Riley thought about it, his hollow belly might have been a contributing factor as to why the allegedly fake wine had hit him so hard.

"Yeah, me, too," he agreed. "Hangovers tend to make me ravenous." Again, he leveled a steady gaze on her, daring her to contradict him.

Not surprisingly, she did. "How could you be hungover?" she asked, her gaze darting over to the stove. Hastily, she moved in that direction, set her coffee on the counter, and made a big production out of turning the bacon in the skillet. "You didn't have anything to drink that would make you hungover. Unless, of course, you were lit up when you got here."

He uttered a ripe curse under his breath. "Not bloody likely," he told her. "I'm not much of a drinker. And notorious howling Barkers or not, I wouldn't have been out driving around last night if I'd been imbibing. I don't know if you've heard, but that's against the law."

She still didn't look at him. "Do tell."

"So, it must have been something I had here."

She lifted a shoulder and let it drop, then turned to a half-dozen eggs that sat at attention in a cardboard carton on the counter. "Well, I'm afraid that's just impossible," she said with a little sigh.

"Where's the bottle?" he asked.

He wasn't sure, but he thought she stiffened. "What bottle?"

"The bottle for that *Château de l'Imposteur,* or whatever the hell it was you called it. Where is it?"

Still not looking at him, she said, "It's in the garbage."

"And where's the garbage?"

"In the big compactor behind the manager's office. I took it out a little while ago. Before you woke up."

He nodded, not surprised. "Mighty convenient, you doing that. There's no way I could retrieve the evidence now, is there?"

"Evidence?" she echoed as she tonged the bacon out of the skillet and onto a paper towel. "My goodness, Sheriff, you sound like you think I've been lying to you."

"Imagine that," he retorted. Before she could comment, and none too sure why he did it, he added, "And I thought I told you to call me Riley. I do remember that part of last night, anyway. That, and the part about you asking me to call you Sabrina."

Her cheeks flushed pink again. "And here I am fixing breakfast for you, Riley," she added as she cracked an egg into the frying pan. "Some guest you are. See if I ever let you fall asleep on my settee again, with or without being sideswiped by the flu."

A twinge of sheepish embarrassment wound through him at that. He supposed he *could* have been coming down with a touch of something last night, something that still had him feeling a might bit under the weather. And he supposed he *was* being awfully grouchy this morning. Funny, but he usually woke up in a pretty good mood. Of course, he usually woke up alone, too, not with some bewitchingly beautiful woman—a woman whose every word had him questioning reality—making him his favorite breakfast.

With a restless sound, he shoved away his doubts about Sabrina for the time being, and, very, very carefully, he stood, still clutching his coffee like a lifeline. Once more, he plowed his fingers through his hair and rubbed a vigorous hand over his jaw. But the gestures did nothing to chase away the muddiness of his thoughts.

"Do you, uh..." he began reluctantly. "I mean, I really hate to ask, but..."

She glanced up, her expression puzzled. "But what?"

Riley inhaled deeply and released the breath slowly. When he did, he noticed that Sabrina dropped her gaze to his chest, where it lingered for some time. "Uh..." he tried again.

"Yes?" she asked.

He cleared his throat with some difficulty, and finally, she returned her gaze to his face. "Do you mind if I...if I use your shower?" he asked, nearly choking on the words.

He really didn't want to take a shower within, oh, say, a million billion trillion miles of Sabrina Jensen, especially with her eyeing him in that hungry way she was right now. But he honestly didn't think he could drive out of here, either, until he did something to wake himself up a little more. And although a sharp stick in the eye would be preferable to being naked in this trailer—unless, of course, Sabrina Jensen was naked with him—Riley really felt the need to clean himself up.

"The shower?" she repeated, panic evident in her voice.

Hell, he might as well have just asked her if she'd like to join him there. And although the thought did have some merit... "I'd just like to get under a hot spray of water for a bit," he said, leaving out the part about having her join him there. "Won't be but a minute."

"But your breakfast," she started to object.

"You go on and have that yourself. I can fix myself something when I get out."

"But—"

"I'll leave plenty of hot water for you, I promise."

Her cheeks turned pink again, as if she were thinking exactly the same thing he was thinking. Namely, that if the two of them showered together, they wouldn't have to worry about conserving much of anything—water, energy, daylight, sexual hunger, whatever.

"O-okay," she stammered.

He waited for her to say more—maybe ask something along the lines of whether or not he'd need help scrubbing his back—but nothing more was forthcoming. So Riley turned and made his way back to the tiny bathroom, trying not to notice that it was right by the bedroom, where Sabrina Jensen's bed was still unmade and rumpled, and wouldn't it be fun to have her all unmade and rumpled, too, right beneath him, while he—

"Towels are in the cabinet under the sink," she called out after him, interrupting his daydream and softening the hard ridge that had started to spring up beneath the zipper of his jeans.

"Thanks," he called over his shoulder. No way was he turning around to face her in this condition.

He leapt into the bathroom and slammed the door shut behind him, leaning back against it to catch his breath. The little enclosure was redolent of some sweet-smelling fragrance—lavender, if Riley wasn't mistaken. His sister used to wear something similar. It occurred to him that just this morning, Sabrina Jensen had been naked in this very spot, and just like that, he was hard again. Man, even hungover, his body was ready to party. No woman had ever gotten such a rise out of Riley before. What was it about Sabrina that made him react this way?

Don't even think about it, he told himself. Best just to put that woman right out of his head, now and forever. Otherwise, he was destined to find himself chest-high in enough trouble for a hundred men. Or certainly four. Him, and the three who were in the running for a claim on Sabrina Jensen's baby. And likewise in the running for a claim on Sabrina Jensen's heart.

Pushing the thought away, Riley reached for the buttons on his shirt and methodically freed them, one by one. A hot shower, he told himself. A big breakfast. Another cup of coffee. Then he'd be ready. Ready to ask Sabrina a few more questions.

He only hoped she was ready to answer them.

Six

Rachel had just swallowed the last bite of her breakfast when she heard the shower shut off in the bathroom. In an effort to speed Riley's departure—and likewise hasten her own peace of mind—she moved hastily into the kitchen to get his breakfast started for him. She had lit the fire and was spreading a third strip of bacon into the skillet, when he exited the bathroom. She glanced up to see him emerge in a puff of steam, his wet hair slicked back, his face and chest still dewy from his shower, his shirt in his hand, and his blue jeans not quite all the way buttoned.

Those last two observations in particular had her engaging in a quick double take, because she wanted to be sure she'd seen what she thought she'd seen—namely, a wet, half-naked, very attractive man standing virtually within grabbing distance.

Yep, that's what she'd seen, all right. Uh-oh.

Which led to a not-so-quick triple take. Because Riley Hunter *out* of his sheriff's duds—and out of his cowboy duds, too, for that matter—was way yummier than Riley Hunter *in* his sheriff's duds, and he'd been pretty way yummy in those. If Rachel had thought him irresistible before—and she *had* thought him irresistible before—then now she was at a complete loss as to what to do.

Actually, that wasn't quite true. She realized pretty quickly that there were in fact quite a few things that she wanted to do, starting with tasting the smooth, umber skin of his chest, followed by kissing that dreamy hollow at the base of his throat, then running her fingers through his wet hair as she fastened her mouth to his, after which she could unfasten what few buttons of his jeans were fastened and then—

Rachel squeezed her eyes shut tight. No. She could do none of those things. She might dream about doing them all she wanted—and even if she didn't want, because there was little chance that the image of Riley Hunter wet and half-naked would be leaving her anytime soon...or ever—but she could not *do* anything. Except maybe suffer a lot.

Swallowing hard, she forced her eyes open, just in time to see Riley holding up his shirt for her inspection. "Sorry," he murmured in a soft, sexy voice. "It was just so steamy in there, I was having trouble drying off and getting dressed."

Oh, and like it wasn't steamy out here, Rachel thought, tugging lightly at the neck of her sweatshirt. "No problem," she lied. "That happens to me all the time. The, uh, the steamy bathroom and not being able to get dressed stuff, I mean."

Briefly, at her assertion, a look crossed his face that indicated he was wishing she hadn't said that. But when he met her gaze again, the look was gone, and his expression was shuttered.

"Just give me a minute," he said. "It's nice and warm out here. I'll dry up in no time."

Well, that made one of them. Because Rachel was fairly certain it was going to be a *looong* time before this damp, hot, heavy, lusty, moist, wet...uh, where was she? Oh, yeah. It was going to be a *looong* time before she felt, uh, dry, again.

"Why don't you come over here in the kitchen where it's warmer?" she asked, mentally smacking her forehead at the stupidity of the question. Having Riley in the kitchen—and, therefore, close enough for her to wrestle him to the ground and have her way with him—was the last thing she needed.

He seemed surprised by her suggestion, then shrugged, as if he intended to take her up on it. Her throat closed up as she watched him approach. Honestly, how any man could make every muscle in his chest dance—*dance*—just by walking was beyond her. But somehow, Riley managed to do just that. In fact, so focused was Rachel on the choreography of his anatomy, that she didn't pay attention to where she was putting the next piece of bacon. Not until she inadvertently tried to drape it over the side of the skillet, and ended up skimming the tender skin of her wrist along the outside of the extremely hot frying pan.

"Ouch!" she cried, dropping the bacon into the open flame of the gas burner. Instinctively, she reached out to extract it, only to have the ball of her hand pass directly over the flame. "Ouch!" she echoed, louder this time. "Oh, *ouch-ouch-ouch-ouch-ouch-ouch-ouch...*"

She dropped the bacon onto the floor and somehow found the presence of mind to shut off the burner. Then she thrust her injured hand into her good one, lifted it to her lips and began to blow on the wounded appendage, as if that would do some good.

Before she realized what was happening, Riley was beside her, carefully turning her burned hand into his to inspect the damage. The flesh of her wrist was red and angry-looking, the ball of her hand pink and puffy. After one look, he pushed her backward toward the sink, spun the cold faucet until water gushed from the spigot, and then shoved her hand under the icy spray.

The relief was instant, but Rachel realized then that it wasn't just her burned hand and wrist that were bothering her. No, in fact, just about everywhere that Riley was touching her—which was a good number of places, thanks to the way he'd thrust his entire body up against hers—she felt an odd sensation fizzing just under her skin, a strange warmth that had nothing to do with her close encounter of the skillet kind.

She watched in fascination as he cradled her smaller hand in both of his bigger ones, withdrawing it from the water long enough to press his fingers tenderly against her wounded flesh. Evidently not quite satisfied that she was okay, he placed her hand back under the cold rush of water, turning it first this way, then that, focused entirely on the injury.

No man could possibly be as gentle as Riley Hunter was, she

marveled. Especially one who was as big and masculine as he was. Yet somehow, she knew that *gentle* was a word that suited him perfectly. She was about to say something to that effect when he glanced up at her and prevented her announcement.

"I don't think it's that bad," he told her. "But it might not hurt to have a doctor look at it, you being pregnant and all."

She smiled at his obvious concern. "I don't think a little burn to my wrist is going to hurt the baby," she said. Hey, how could it? The baby was probably hundreds of miles away by now. She pulled her hand out of the water and studied her wrist, flexing her fingers as she made a few quick circular motions with her hand. "See? Good as new."

But Riley wasn't satisfied. With that endearing gentleness, he dried her hand off with a nearby dish towel, then held it in both of his again. "Looks like you might wind up with a blister," he said, sawing his thumb carefully over the sensitive flesh on her wrist.

With each soft motion of his fingertip, an explosion went off in Rachel's midsection, and her pulse leapt higher. Evidently, he noticed the quick rush of her heart rate beneath his thumb, because when he glanced up again, his eyes were darker, the black pupils nearly eclipsing the bittersweet chocolate of his irises.

"You sure you're okay?" he asked, his voice quieter, huskier than it had been before.

She nodded, but couldn't quite summon the strength to say anything out loud. Which was just as well, because her thoughts were so muddled at the moment, she had no idea what to say.

"Your, uh, your pulse," he added, "your heart... It, uh, it seems to be pounding pretty fierce."

Instinctively, Rachel lifted her free hand to spread it open over the center of her chest, double-checking his assessment of her heart rate. Sure enough, she felt it galloping beneath her fingertips like a herd of wild stallions. But then, that was hardly a surprise, seeing as how her blood was roaring in her ears, and she was growing dizzier and dizzier by the moment.

"I...you...we...uh..." she stammered. "That...that just startled me, is all. Getting burned, I mean. By the skillet, I mean."

This time he was the one to nod without speaking.

Although she had no idea what possessed her to do it, Rachel moved her hand to Riley's still bare chest, and she splayed her fingers open over his heart, as she had just done to her own seconds before. And just as her heart had been then, his was raging behind his rib cage at a phenomenal, albeit irregular, speed. She smiled, somehow relieved by the fact that he would be as agitated as she was, that he would be as terrified of what had just happened—of what was happening still—as she.

"You, uh," she began again, "your heart seems to be doing a few double flips, too."

For one long moment, neither of them said a word, but stood perfectly still in the tiny kitchen, staring at each other. Riley held her hand in his, and his thumb continued to move over her wrist with a languid, random motion, back...and...forth, back...and...forth, back...and...forth. And Rachel continued to press her hand against the smooth, heated flesh of his chest, her fingers curling and uncurling with much the same kind of movement.

Then, at exactly the same moment, as if orchestrated by a master composer, each reached for the other. As Riley curved the fingers of one hand around her nape, Rachel scooted her hand across his chest and up to his naked shoulder. Together, each pulled the other closer, until nothing more separated them than a scant breath of air. And then, even that small barrier ceased to exist, because, with one swift, graceful motion, he bent forward and covered her mouth with his.

It was an extraordinary kiss, quite unlike anything Rachel had ever experienced before. Although, granted, it had been a long, long time since she'd let a man get close enough to kiss her. Still... This kiss was a lot different from those she had enjoyed early in her dating history. A *lot* different.

He began by brushing his lips lightly over hers...once, twice, three times...caresses so soft, so brief, that for a moment she had to wonder if he'd kissed her at all. He nuzzled her nose with his and rubbed his cheek gently over hers, then parted his lips and dragged them lightly over her cheek, her jaw, her throat. For a moment, he withdrew to take a step closer, bringing his body flush with hers. He hesitated only long enough to gaze down into her eyes, then tilted his head slightly to the right and dipped it forward, slanting his mouth over hers again.

Oh, yeah, Rachel thought. Definitely different.

This time when Riley kissed her, he put himself into it completely—body and soul. As he claimed her mouth and tongue with his, he pushed himself forward, the hand at her nape bunching her hair in his fist, the other weaving his fingers together with hers at her waist. Urging both their arms behind her, he virtually wrapped himself around Rachel, rendering her nearly helpless—not that she necessarily wanted any help. Then, slowly, deliberately, seductively, he walked them both backward until the refrigerator halted their progress.

And then, with a heartfelt groan, Riley crowded his big body into hers, crushing himself into Rachel as if he intended to join them as one. He insinuated one of his legs between hers, using his strong thigh to spread hers open, lifting it high enough so that the most intimate part of her was straddling him. Acting solely on instinct, and before she realized what she was doing, Rachel thrust her hips forward to meet him.

Immediately, she regretted the gesture. Because the friction of his muscular thigh rubbing insistently against such an inexperienced part of her roused a hunger, an absolute need, inside her that she hadn't been aware existed. From some place deep within, a long, lusty groan escaped her. Then, wanting—needing—more, she moved her hips backward, and then forward, again. And again. And again. And again.

With one final push of her hips against his, Rachel felt Riley swell to life, and she nearly collapsed against him at the absolute power she detected in him. As if he sensed her instability, he shifted his leg higher, pushing it even more intimately against her, driving her breath from her lungs in a long, hot whoosh of air. She told herself she should be frightened by the suddenness and intensity of what was happening between them, that she should put a halt to it immediately, before things went beyond her control. Instead, with every passing moment, she only grew more and more excited, more and more intent on making Riley her own.

She moved the hand at his shoulder into his hair, wrapping a handful of the long tresses around her fingers before cupping his head in her palm and pushing him forward for a more thorough plunder of her mouth. This time, Rachel was the one to take control of the kiss, and she used the opportunity to explore every inch of him that she could find. He tasted of coffee and heat, smelled of soap and man. Beneath her fingertips, his skin became hot and alive everywhere she touched him. The sound of his breathing was a rush of ragged wind that mimicked her own rough respiration, and the feel of him surrounding her was an inescapable lure.

When she felt his hand pressing over her hip, she realized he had released her other hand. So she brought it up to cup his jaw, and discovered as she kissed him again that his face was as smooth and warm as his chest had been. That realization evaporated quickly, though, when the hand at her hip moved higher. Riley dipped his fingers beneath the waistband of her sweatshirt, skimming them over the bare skin just above her blue jeans. Rachel stilled at the exquisite tenderness of the gesture, and she held her breath to see what he would do next.

What he did next was scoot his hand higher, his fingers tripping delicately over her rib cage as if he were playing the most fragile of musical instruments. Only when he encountered the small swell of her breast did his hand cease its progress. But he didn't quite retreat. Instead, he cradled the lower curve of her breast in the ample L-shaped valley of his thumb and forefinger. Then he paused, as if he were waiting for her okay before he proceeded any further.

Slowly, softly, sweetly, Rachel ended the kiss, but instead of pulling away, she dipped her head into the curve where his neck and shoulder joined. Feeling inexplicably shy all of a sudden, she only curled her body into his, splaying one hand open over his naked chest, curving the other open over his naked shoulder. When she turned her head to press a soft kiss to the strong column of his throat, Riley, without warning, covered her breast with his hand and squeezed gently, possessively. Her nipple peaked beneath the scant lace of her bra, and through the filmy fabric, he stroked her with the pad of his thumb.

"Oh," she murmured softly. "Oh, Riley..."

At that moment, it hit Rachel with crystal clear acuity that whatever was happening now with Riley felt different from her other experiences with men because it *was* different. She didn't know why, or how it had come about, but there it was just the same. Somehow, suddenly, what was happening between them just felt...right. Natural. Good. As if it were meant to be.

So what if she'd fallen in love with Riley as easily as she'd fallen in love with a score of other men? she thought dreamily. So what if he'd charmed her and seduced her in no time at all? So what if the conditions that had thrown them together were less than ideal? Less than reasonable? Less than normal?

It was different this time, she told herself. It *was.* She knew it was. She could feel it. There was no reason on earth why she and Riley couldn't just continue down this path right now, to see where it ultimately led them. No reason why they should try to call a stop to what was clearly an inevitable outcome. No reason why she couldn't just give herself over to him, right here, right now, utterly and completely, mind, body and—

"Sabrina," he said, his voice a quiet murmur of needing and wanting that pierced her to her very soul.

Rachel's eyes snapped open as her dream evaporated like so much fairy dust. Suddenly, she remembered that there was, in fact, a reason—a really good one, too—why she and Riley couldn't continue with what was clearly *not* such an inevitable outcome. There was the small matter of him thinking she was someone else entirely. The small matter of her having lied to him since the moment she laid eyes on him. The small matter that the entire foundation for their coming together was one big, fat fabrication.

Okay, so maybe there *was* a little hitch, she thought, sighing disconsolately at the realization.

"Uh..." she began.

But anything she had been about to say was halted there, because Riley chose that moment to push his open palm expertly across her breast, to dip his head to her neck and brush his lips lightly over her heated flesh. The thigh thrust between hers shifted just the tiniest bit, just enough to send her blood zinging throughout her entire system. And that was when Rachel *finally* came to her senses.

She had to put a stop to this immediately. Riley was under the impression that he had someone else in his arms, a woman who was pregnant, lost and alone, a woman he wanted to protect and care for. And, simply put, Rachel was nowhere near being that woman. Who knew how Riley would be reacting now if he knew the truth? There was a good chance that the only reason he wanted her at the moment was because he saw her as a vulnerable woman who needed someone to lean on.

There were a lot of guys who went for that kind of woman, she knew. A lot of guys who liked to cast themselves in the position of caretaker. Rachel, however, had been taking care of herself for a long time now, and the last thing she needed was a shoulder to lean on. Well, usually, she amended reluctantly. But if Riley knew that about her, knew she didn't need him the way a woman in Sabrina's position might, if he knew who she really was, would he still be holding her close this way? Or would a woman who didn't need his help and protection be a complete turnoff to him?

With that sobering realization came another, the realization that Rachel had more than likely been kidding herself if she thought for a moment that what was happening between her and Riley was in any way different from anything she'd experienced with a man in the past.

She'd fallen fast and hard for a beautiful face and a charming manner, she reminded herself. How did that differ from her past experiences? Oh, sure, she'd let Riley kiss her and caress her and drive her to near madness, something that hadn't exactly been par for her dating course before now. But if she thought things would work out differently with him than they had with anyone else, she was just plain crazy. Or stupid. Or both.

How could she have let herself be fooled that way? she demanded of herself. How could she have let things between them accelerate to the point of such intimacy? How could she have let herself believe this was different? The only thing different with Riley was that she'd allowed things to go too far.

Stupid, stupid, stupid, she chastised herself.

With no small effort, Rachel released Riley's hair and shoulders and moved her hands to his chest, trying to ignore the warmth and satin softness beneath her fingertips. Not quite able to put voice to her objections, she simply opened her palms and pressed them firmly against him, hoping he'd get the message. For a moment, he didn't move, only kept his leg pressed confidently against the heated core of her, and continued to cup her breast in one hand.

So Rachel pushed a little harder. And then, slowly, gradually, her action must have dawned on him. Because slowly, gradually, Riley released her and took a step away.

Before she could utter a word in explanation, he spun brusquely around, scooping up his shirt from the floor and thrusting his arms into the sleeves in one fluid gesture. All Rachel could do was watch in silence as, with his back turned to her, he buttoned himself up. When he was finished, he strode to the living room and sat down to tug on his boots, all the while ignoring her. And little by little, any hopes she'd entertained that the two of them might salvage a good outcome to the awkward encounter began to crumble away.

"Riley?"

The sound of his name slicing through the silence seemed to surprise them both. Rachel wasn't sure what made her call out to him that way, but once she did, she had no desire to retract the summons, even if she had no idea what she was going to say.

His jerky, vigorous movements slowed when she spoke. But he continued to avoid looking at her, and she began to think he wasn't going to reply. She was about to speak his name again when he finally turned to look at her. But as quickly as his eyes met hers, he dropped his gaze to the floor again.

"I'm sorry," he said, the words choppy, forced, and in no way repentant. "That shouldn't have happened. I apologize for overstepping the bounds of...of...of whatever the boundaries are for people in a situation like this."

Rachel swallowed hard. "And what kind of situation is this?" she asked, in spite of the fact that she knew the answer to that better than he did. She ignored the realization and waited to hear his side of things instead.

"An impossible one, that's what kind," he answered shortly.

And again, although she already knew the answer to her question, she asked anyway, "How is it impossible?"

Riley leveled a gaze on her for a long time before speaking. When he did, it was after expelling a harsh, restless-sounding breath of air. "You oughta know that better than me," he said, putting voice to the very thoughts she'd had circling in her own brain.

"I'd still like to hear your take on things," she told him quietly.

He shook his head slowly. "No, I don't think you would."

"Try me."

The sound he emitted this time was harsher, more menacing than before. "Hell, honey, in case you hadn't noticed, I just did try you."

This time, Rachel was the one to look down at the ground. "Riley, don't...please..."

He said nothing in response to her plea, and when she braved a glance up at him, she found him staring at her with eyes that were cool and distant.

So Rachel tried again. "I'm sorry I—"

He surged from the settee faster than a cyclone, cutting her off. "Oh, no, you don't," he said sharply, settling his hands on his hips. A muscle twitched in his jaw. "Don't you dare apologize for what just happened." He lifted one hand to jab a finger toward the kitchen. "That...that was my fault, not yours. I had no right to...to..."

"To what?" she asked.

He hesitated before answering, two bright spots of pink staining his cheeks. But whether his heightened color was the result of embarrassment or anger or leftover passion, Rachel couldn't have said for sure.

Just when she thought he wasn't going to say anything more, he inhaled deeply and snapped, "I had no right to...to take advantage of a pregnant woman that way."

"To do what?" she asked incredulously, certain she must have misunderstood him.

"You know what I mean, Sabrina."

Rachel shook her head. "No, I don't. Enlighten me."

He growled under his breath, hooked his hands back onto his

hips and glared at her. In spite of his admission to the contrary, he sure did seem to be blaming her for what had happened. Certainly, he was as mad at her as he seemed to be at himself.

"Look, maybe I don't know a lot about pregnant women," he began, his words clipped and quick, "but I do know there's a lot of hormonal...stuff...going on that makes women like you do things you wouldn't normally do otherwise. Like...like..."

She gritted her teeth, pretty sure she knew what was coming next. "Like what?" she demanded.

His color deepened, and he glanced away as he continued, "Like...well...throwing yourself at a perfect stranger. That kind of thing."

Rachel gaped at him. "Throwing myself," she echoed. "You think I threw myself at you in there because my prenatal hormones are all in an uproar and I need some lovin' from whatever man is available?"

He nodded quickly, one time.

"You have *got* to be kidding."

His gaze found its way back to hers long enough to ricochet elsewhere again. In a very quiet voice, he said, "Don't tell me that kind of thing is news to you."

"Oh, I think that would be news to obstetricians and gynecologists everywhere," she countered. "Unlike you, *Dr.* Hunter, I don't think most experts know how hormonal reactions turn pregnant women into stark, raving nymphomaniacs. You should write a paper on the subject."

"That wasn't what I meant."

"Oh, wasn't it?"

He shook his head and finally, finally, met her gaze again. "I just meant that under normal circumstances, that...that..." He sighed heavily. "What happened in the kitchen wouldn't have happened. And since I'm the only one here who's...who's..."

"Normal?" she supplied for him, proud of herself for the fact that she kept herself under control and did *not* pop him in the eye, the way she wanted to. Honestly. Suggesting that a woman went nympho just because she was pregnant. Nauseous, maybe, but not nympho.

"No," he quickly contradicted her. "That wasn't what I meant."

"Then just what did you mean, Riley? Could you at least tell me that?"

He frowned. "I meant that, in your condition, you can't be held accountable for your actions right now, but I sure as hell can be held accountable for mine. And I shouldn't have taken advantage of you that way. I'm sorry, dammit. Can't you just accept my apology and let's be done with it?"

His voice had risen ten decibels with every word he uttered, so by the time he finished, he was shouting loud enough to be heard in Texarkana. His breathing was loud and labored, his body rigid with his anger. And all Rachel could do was marvel at the fact that he was just so daggone cute when he was mad this way.

Shoot. That was the last reaction she should be having.

When she said nothing in response to his outburst, he uttered something unintelligible under his breath that she figured she was better off not hearing anyway. Then he raked both big hands through his still-damp hair and muttered quickly, "I gotta get going."

"But—"

"I gotta check in with Virgil and Rosario," he interrupted as he reached for his jacket. Once again, his movements took on that too rapid, too awkward pace, and he nearly tripped over himself as he crossed to retrieve his hat from the chair.

"They're gonna think I've fallen off the planet," he continued, "and the last time that happened, Rosario sent her sister to check on me. No offense to Consuela, but I don't want to find that woman on my doorstep again with that alleged flu remedy. That stuff smelled like...like... Well, suffice it to say, I think it had some ingredients in it that weren't exactly legal, never mind healthful, and I'd just as soon not put my job in a compromising position like that again, even if it's not the most high-falutin' position in the world. You hear what I'm sayin' here?"

Rachel shook her head. "No. I don't. But you sure do seem to be doing a lot of talking for somebody who's not saying anything. Riley, I think we need to—"

"Be saying goodbye," he finished for her, donning his hat.

"Right you are." In three quick steps, he was at the front door, which he shoved open without preamble and stepped through. As if it were an afterthought, he called over his shoulder without looking back, "And don't forget, Sabrina. You've got until tomorrow to figure out what you're gonna do about the Wentworths. I'll be calling them around suppertime."

And with that, Sheriff Riley Hunter, Wallace Canyon PD, closed the door behind himself. And then all Rachel could do was shake her head in wonder at what had just happened, not to mention at what was still to come.

Seven

At eleven-fifteen Monday morning, Riley was sitting in his office doing what he did every Monday morning—nibbling a Lorna Doone and waiting for something to happen. Well, that, and re-hashing over and over again in his fevered brain what had happened in Sabrina Jensen's trailer the morning before. But, hey, he'd been rehashing that over and over again for more than twenty-four hours now, hadn't he, so what was the big, damned deal? Just because he was no closer to explaining it now than he had been when it happened, that was no reason to be so preoccupied, was it? Shoot.

All he knew now was what he'd known then. That when he'd seen Sabrina burn herself on the stove, every rational thought had fled his brain, to be replaced by an urgency and need to protect unlike anything he'd ever felt before in his life. He'd seen her get hurt, and he'd immediately wanted to help. That was all there was to it. But then something had gone wrong. In addition to wanting to protect Sabrina, he'd suddenly wanted to possess her. And in the most basic, most ancient, most me-man-you-woman-we-mate way available, too.

So much for being the great protector, he thought dismally. The great pouncer was more like it.

He'd just gone too long without any kind of female companionship, that was his problem. Wallace Canyon was short on a lot of things, after all, not the least of which was eligible bachelorettes. The few women in town who were in the vicinity of Riley's age were all married—except, of course, for Eloise Hawkins, who was known throughout the Oklahoma panhandle as being sweet on Virgil Bybee. And all the women in Wallace Canyon who were single were old enough that the only thing they were interested in doing for Riley was baking him the occasional pie.

He sighed and lifted his coffee to his lips for an idle sip, but that only reminded him of that first day with Sabrina, when she'd gone to make him coffee and spilled grounds everywhere, and the two of them had wound up in each other's arms, however unintentionally.

Riley shook his head ruefully. Everything reminded him of Sabrina now. He couldn't shower without recalling the one he took at her place. He couldn't eat breakfast without remembering that she'd been cooking bacon for him when she'd burned herself. He couldn't get dressed without being confronted by the memory of hastily throwing on his clothes at her trailer after their all too heated embrace.

Hell, he couldn't even enjoy a Lorna Doone without being assaulted by the memory of her even, white teeth nibbling a cookie in that Naugahyde chair across from his desk.

In fact, just sitting in his office reminded him of Sabrina now. It was the dangedest thing. Never before had a woman crept up on him the way she had. Somehow, in the short time he'd known her, she'd touched every facet of his life, had imprinted herself on every crack and crevice in his brain, had invaded every body part he possessed. He could still smell the lavender scent of her, could still feel the warmth and softness of her skin, could still taste the bittersweet mixture of coffee and sugar that had lingered on her lips. And somehow, he knew that even if he lived to be a hundred years old, the memory of Sabrina Jensen would never quite fade from his mind.

"Riley! You better come see this! Hurry!"

Virgil's summons bellowed down the hallway before erupting in the office with an urgency Riley couldn't ignore. Surging up from his chair, Lorna Doones and Sabrina Jensen all but forgotten, he raced to follow the sound of his deputy's voice. He found Virgil in the Xerox room—well, what they called the Xerox room, anyway, even if the old copier they had was really a way, way, *way* off brand—staring down at the fax machine with much trepidation. Riley followed the deputy's gaze to find the machine humming and moaning in a way he'd never quite heard it do before.

"I think it's possessed," Virgil said in a whisper, as if he feared the machine would hear him and take offense. "I think we need to call a faxorcist."

Riley turned to look at his deputy through narrowed eyes. "A faxorcist?" he repeated.

"Well, look at it," Virgil went on, still whispering. He took a step backward and to the side, one that placed Riley between his deputy and the allegedly satanic fax machine. "It's never done *that* before."

True enough, Riley concurred. In fact, he couldn't recall ever seeing *any* kind of machine do that. *That* being a shivery dance of unknown origin as it gasped and clattered and... whoa...

sparked, sputtered and smoked. As one unit, he and Virgil took a step backward. Then another, and another, and another, until the two men stood on the opposite side of the Xerox room, backs against the wall, as if awaiting execution. But still the fax machine growled and jerked, another thin thread of smoke uncurling from the back.

"Go unplug it," Riley instructed his deputy, dropping his own voice in what he assured himself was *not* an effort to keep the fax machine from hearing. He was just being polite, that was all.

Virgil shook his shaggy, blond head adamantly. "Uh-uh. No way. I'm not gonna go unplug it. You go unplug it."

Riley glared at him. "Virgil, I gave you an order."

"I don't care, Riley. I'm not going anywhere near that thing. I have a date with Eloise tonight."

Riley rolled his eyes. *Boy, you want something done right,* he thought.

Resting his hand on the butt of his pistol—well, you just never knew—he took a few tentative steps forward. But the fax machine started uttering some truly bizarre—and, he had to admit, somewhat satanic—sounds, so he hesitated, unsnapping his holster. Instead of abating at Riley's clear threat to shoot, however, the machine's grating and grinding only intensified, as did the sparks and smoke. Just when Riley thought he was indeed going to have to draw his weapon and put the fax machine out of its misery, it gurgled one final time, wheezed out a couple of spastic breaths, and then...

And then started spewing forth not pea soup, but a long sheet of flimsy paper that seemed to go on forever. For several long moments, the fax machine regurgitated information, the paper piling on the floor in a messy heap. Then, finally, as if its work on this good, green earth was done, the fax machine gasped its last and died.

For a minute, Riley and Virgil only stood staring at its smoking remains without speaking. Then slowly, carefully, Virgil made his way to the machine and tore off the paper dangling from its exit wound. Evidently none too certain of the fax machine's demise, however, the deputy quickly skittered back to the other side of the room. So Riley refastened his holster and followed, nodding toward the paper in question.

"What's that?" he asked his deputy wryly. "Its last will and testament?"

Virgil shook his head slowly as he read over the paper's contents, clearly lost in thought. "No. Looks like this is all the little bits and pieces of stuff that never quite made it through the fax over the last few years."

"You're kidding."

Virgil shook his head again. "Nope. Looky here." He thumbed one paragraph in particular. "This here's the rest of that recipe for wassail that Rosario wanted last Christmas. She asked Lynette Parmentier over in Felt to fax it to her, but only the first half ever got here. Boy, was Rosario mad when that thing came through without listing all the spices she needed."

Virgil glanced up from his reading material and gave Riley a knowing look. "And just between you and me, Riley," he added parenthetically, "when Rosario took it upon herself to substitute with chili peppers and jalapenos... Well, let's just say that last year's Christmas party here at the station was *not* without its aftermath."

Riley expelled an impatient sound and somehow refrained from rolling his eyes. "Is there anything there that we might deem, oh...I don't know...*important?*" he asked.

Virgil read further as he pulled the length of paper through his fingers. "Well, now, let me check... We've got last month's scores from the Wallace Canyon High School-Montrose Academy football homecoming game." He turned to Riley again, his expression afire. "Boy, that was a close one, Riley. You shoulda been there. Talk about your grudge match. And that little Roberta Salvos is one helluva lineman. She just about—"

"Virgil," Riley interrupted him.

His deputy squinted at him for a minute as if he couldn't quite understand why Riley would cut off what promised to be the sports anecdote of the season. Then, finally, it must have dawned on him that there were one or two other matters of significance that might be in the fax's remains.

"Oh," he murmured, glancing back down at the paper. "Oh, sorry. Uh, let me see..." He shook his head as he read. "Nothing much here that appears to be recent. Oh, wait a second. Maybe there is. Here's what looks like...yep, it is. It's the rest of that updated APB on Sabrina Jensen that didn't come through on Friday."

Riley snatched the paper from Virgil's hand. "Lemme see that."

Not that it would tell him anything he didn't already know, he thought. There couldn't possibly be anything in that updated APB about how soft Sabrina Jensen's hair was, or how good she smelled, or how her smile just lit up brighter than a Christmas tree, or anything like that. Quickly, he scanned the information, from bottom to top, working his way backward.

Nope. Nothing about how wonderful she was or how good it felt to hold her in your arms or how she could turn a man inside out just by walking into the same room. Only more of the stuff about her being missing for months...working as a waitress, which was obviously wrong, because Sabrina had told him she was a bartender...her last and previous known locations...and that she was due to deliver her baby in—

February.

Riley read over that part of the APB again, just to be sure he'd done it right the first time. Yep, he had. In fact, as he read over the updated version again, paying closer attention to the specific words this time, in addition to listing her due date as February, the APB mentioned in two other places that the missing woman was seven months pregnant. So there was no way the information could have resulted from a misprint or a typo. There was no question that Sabrina Jensen was seven months along. And even a fool would know that a woman who was seven months along would be showing by now, right? Certainly she wouldn't have the flat, enticing little tummy that the woman living out in the Westport Trailer Park had. The woman who had *said* she was Sabrina Jensen. The woman who *looked* like Sabrina Jensen.

The woman who obviously *wasn't* Sabrina Jensen.

Well, well, well. Now wasn't *this* an interesting little bit of news?

"Virgil," Riley said as he headed out the door, "can you handle things here for a little while? I've got to go out for a bit."

"Sure thing, Riley," his deputy assured him with a puzzled expression. "But what's the hurry? Where's the fire?"

Riley smiled grimly. "No fire yet," he said evenly. "But there sure as hell is gonna be one. Just as soon as I can get myself over to the Westport Trailer Park. The minute I get my hands on whoever that woman is pretending to be Sabrina Jensen."

Rachel was slipping batch number four of the Christmas cookies—nut nibbles, her favorite—off of a bent and battered cookie sheet when she heard the now familiar grumble of Riley Hunter's utility vehicle outside Sabrina's trailer. She'd spent the first part of her morning making phone calls to the last of the people she could think of who might have heard from Sabrina. Then, feeling restless as she waited for a number of people to call back, she'd resorted to an old familiar pastime to ease her anxiety.

There wasn't a lot in life that Rachel was good at, but baking was one thing she had mastered early on, something on which she fell back whenever she needed to ease the pressures of living her day-to-day life. And Christmas naturally always brought out the baking gene full force. Cookies were what she gave to *everybody* on her list for Christmas, from the mail carrier to her hairstylist to her regular customers at the restaurant.

She'd estimated she could finish a half dozen batches of several different kinds of Christmas cookies before she was due at the police station that afternoon, and she'd intended to take some with her when she went. She'd figured that a tin of Christmas cookies would be something she could leave behind for Riley to enjoy once she came clean with the truth, retrieved her car keys, and left for Oklahoma City in the morning.

Because it looked as though that was exactly what Rachel was going to have to do. Tell Riley the truth, apologize for lying to him, then go back home with her tail between her legs to wait for word from—and worry about—Sabrina.

Although once Riley realized the extent of her dishonesty, the last thing he would want would be any reminders of his time with Rachel, she'd thought maybe—just maybe—he might like a little something to remember her by. Doubtful, but possible, she knew. And seeing as how he was such a big fan of cookies, maybe a few dozen would go a long way toward earning some small forgiveness for her deception. Though at this point, she doubted Riley would ever forgive her completely.

She sighed heavily as she scooted the spatula under two nut nibbles at once. It sure was going to be a blue Christmas this year, she thought. She'd already been dreading it with Sabrina on the run—and with the prospect of telling her father about her sister's situation hanging on the horizon—because Rachel always got together with her sister and father for the holidays. They all took turns hosting each other, and this year it had been Rachel's turn to have the holiday at her apartment.

She'd gone out of her way to make the place festive, too. She'd bought a big ol' Fraser fir that was probably going bone dry while she sat here in Wallace Canyon. She'd strung lights around every window, garland around every door. She'd even hung mistletoe, just for the fun of it. And she'd stuffed her refrigerator to the gills with eggnog and mulled cider and party sausages and cheese balls.

She had done all that, because Christmas was the one time of the year when her family could get together and be a family, no matter what might have kept them apart through the year. But this year would be different. This year would be no fun at all. With Christmas a week away, something told Rachel that Sabrina wouldn't be drinking eggnog with her and their father come Christmas Eve night. She just hoped her sister found herself a nice place to hole up for the holiday. Nobody should be alone at Christmas time.

Strangely, that realization made Rachel think of Riley, because now, in addition to Sabrina's absence, she was going to feel his. And she couldn't help but wonder if maybe he'd be missing her come Christmas Eve, too. Right now, she even felt like Riley's absence would probably be more noticeable than Sabrina's. And not just on Christmas, either.

At least Sabrina had called from time to time over the last few months to let Rachel know she was safe. And Rachel was confident that eventually Sabrina would work out her problems, and the two of them, and their father, would be together again. Come hell or high water, Sabrina would doubtless telephone them on Christmas, regardless of where she was, to wish them a happy holiday and let them know she was safe.

Riley, on the other hand...

Well, Rachel figured it was a pretty safe bet that she wouldn't be seeing or hearing from Riley ever again. Because once he found out how badly she'd been lying to him, once he realized she wasn't the woman he thought she was, then he wasn't going to want to have anything to do with her. Period.

Which she supposed was just as well, anyway. It wasn't as if they had any future together. Even if she was feeling heartsick about leaving.

All she could do now was look forward to going back to Oklahoma City and finding a job—hopefully before the end of the year—so that she could meet some handsome, charming, superficial man who would flirt with her and sweep her off her feet for a few hours, and make her forget all about Riley Hunter. Because that was all it was going to take to make her forget about him. Someone else. Someone new.

She hoped.

No, not hoped, she corrected herself. Knew. She knew that was all it would take to purge Riley from her head and her heart once and for all. Another beautiful face. That was what Rachel needed now.

As if conjured by the thought, the silhouette of Riley's beautiful face beneath the outline of his Stetson appeared at Sabrina's front door. Before Rachel could call out to him, however, he began to slam his fist against the door, a good half dozen times, at least, hard enough to shake the whole trailer.

Startled by the fierceness of his pounding, and still scooting cookies off the cookie sheet, Rachel didn't answer right away. And when she finally collected herself and did try to call out, to tell him to just hold his horses for a minute, for crying out loud, a burst of sound erupted out of nowhere, immediately followed by the crash of the front door as it slammed inward and onto the ground.

Oh...my...God, Rachel thought as the cookie sheet clattered to the floor and she leapt backward. She gaped, shaking her head in amazement, when she realized that Riley had kicked the front door in, had knocked it right off its hinges. And then she didn't have time to think at all, because he entered the trailer and completely filled it.

"Riley, what on earth do you think you're—" Her words were cut off when she noted the absolute rage that glittered in his eyes.

She didn't think she'd ever seen anyone exude so much anger, so much bitterness, so much raw power than Sheriff Riley Hunter did at that moment. She opened her mouth to speak again, but any words she might be capable of rousing got scared, and then stuck in her windpipe. She swallowed in an effort to free them, but to no avail. All that emerged was an anxious little squeak. Then even that was squelched when Riley began to move forward.

Talk about being stalked, she thought. Maybe she ought to call the police....

She licked her lips nervously and took a step backward, but all that did was bump her into the counter. Briefly, she pondered the possibility of squeezing through the tiny window over the sink, but seeing as how she'd consumed a good dozen cookies in the last hour, she figured her hips would never make it. So she stood motionless, watching Riley as he watched her, panicking with every step he took forward to dissolve the distance between them.

"Miss Jensen?" he growled, his words dripping with contempt. Funny, but he'd said her name without even moving his lips or jaw.

In spite of the fact that he clearly knew now that she wasn't who she had claimed to be, Rachel swallowed hard and nodded.

"Miss *Sabrina* Jensen?" he asked further.

For one insane moment, Rachel thought about trying to perpetuate the charade and swear up and down that yes, she was Sabrina Jensen, as a matter of fact, and how could she help the good sheriff, and hadn't they already had this conversation once?

But reason, which she knew really should have stepped in days ago, finally intervened. It was pretty obvious Riley had learned something since yesterday that he hadn't known before, and somehow Rachel was certain she'd be in much bigger trouble than she was already if she tried to lie to him again.

So, slowly, silently, she shook her head.

"You're *not* Sabrina Jensen?" he asked, his voice laced with a mixture of triumph and disgust.

Again, she shook her head, but said nothing.

"Who are you then?" he asked further. "Her evil twin?"

Rachel licked her dry lips, swallowed a few more times and tried to smile. Naturally, she didn't even come close to achieving one. "Um, something like that, yeah," she finally replied. "Not her evil twin, actually, just, uh...her...her well-intentioned twin?"

Riley continued to eye her venomously. "You're Sabrina Jensen's twin sister?"

She nodded. "Well-intentioned twin sister," she elaborated again.

Still he looked skeptical. "Got any ID?"

"Yes. In my wallet."

She took a step to the left, to move around him, only to have her foot land on the cookie sheet she'd dropped earlier. A cookie sheet which was now surrounded by a scattering of quickly cooling—and pretty much crushed beyond recognition—nut nibbles. Her favorites. Daggone it.

"Oh, now, will you just look at that?" she demanded, momentarily forgetting that Riley Hunter was *this* close to doing something rash to her person. "What is it with you?" she continued, still not looking at him. "Every time you come around, you make me drop something."

"Maybe it's not me who makes you drop things," he stated evenly. "Maybe it's your guilty liar's conscience."

Oops. She'd forgotten about that. Well, yeah, it could be her guilty liar's conscience, she thought. Or it could just be the way he made her entire body do a little erotic dance that would probably be illegal in some states.

Instead of commenting, she hastily stooped to clear away the mess, discarding the remnants of the ruined batch on the counter. When she straightened, she found Riley staring at her, and she couldn't figure out why.

"Your ID?" he asked her again, jogging her memory.

"Oh, yeah."

Once more, she took a step to the left, to move around Riley and retrieve her purse from Sabrina's bedroom. But he followed her action with a step to his right, so that he continued to block her way. Frowning, Rachel moved to the right, only to have him step deftly to his left. So she went left again. And Riley went right.

"Well, it's gonna be kind of hard to get my wallet if you keep dancing with me this way," she said, exasperated.

For a moment, he only continued to stare at her, then, finally, he stepped aside. Rachel hesitated a moment, worried that this might be another trap, then took a tentative step around him. This time he didn't move at all. Not until she had just squeaked by him. Then he snaked out a hand and circled her wrist with firm fingers.

"Don't be trying anything funny," he cautioned her.

As if, she thought. Aloud, she said, "Like what?"

"Like bolting through that door and stealing my vehicle," he told her. "I'd just love an excuse to haul your butt down to the station and lock it up with the rest of you."

She glared at him, her anger compounding, even if she was the one who was responsible for Riley's reaction. "You know, I hadn't thought about doing that," she said, "but now that you mention it..."

"Don't even think about it."

"I wasn't," she insisted. "I just told you I wasn't. You're the one who brought it up. Sheesh."

"Sabri—" He expelled a dissatisfied sound. "Miss Jensen," he corrected himself. "About that ID...?"

"I'm working on it, if you'll just give me a chance."

He released her wrist and let her pass, but not before admonishing her, "Seems I already gave you a chance. And look how that turned out."

Rachel felt her face flame, but she kept moving until she'd retrieved her purse from Sabrina's bedroom. "I can explain that," she said as she returned to the kitchen, rifling through her purse.

"Oh, I'm just on pins and needles waiting to hear that explanation," he countered. "Something tells me it involves UFOs, genetic mutants and Mr. Elvis Presley himself."

Rachel ignored him. "Here," she said, thrusting her driver's license at him. "See? I really am Sabrina's sister."

"Rachel Jensen," he said, scowling. "Okay, so the two of you have the same last name. Big deal."

"And the same face," she pointed out. "And the same birthdate."

"I don't know Sabrina's birthdate. Only that she's twenty-four."

"And so am I."

Without responding, he glanced back down at the grainy photo on her driver's license. Grudgingly, he said, "I gotta admit that you do look exactly like the photo we got of your...of Sabrina Jensen, that's for sure."

"Yeah, well identical twins do generally bear an uncanny resemblance to each other," she said dryly. "Funny how it works out that way every single time. That must be why they're referred to as 'identical.'"

He ignored her sarcasm. "So, if you're Rachel Jensen, then where the hell is Sabrina?" he asked when he glanced up at her again.

She met his intense gaze levelly. "I wish I knew."

"My guess is that you *do* know. You just don't want to tell me."

"Then you're guessing wrong."

They were nearly nose to nose by now, so angry had each become at the other. Riley was obviously ticked off because of Rachel's deception and dishonesty, and Rachel was mad because...because... Well, because Riley still didn't seem to believe her, even though she was telling the truth now. She didn't like being mistrusted by him. Even if she had done an awful lot of stuff that commanded mistrust.

"I think, Miss Rachel Jensen," Riley said curtly, "that you oughta come down to the station with me again. I suddenly have a whole bunch more questions to ask you."

She shook her head. "Not this time. You want to talk to me, you'll do it here."

He placed one hand on a hip he jutted to the side, the other—the one still fingering her driver's license—on the butt of his pistol. It was a stance Rachel duly noted. "Oh, will I?" he said through gritted teeth.

Feeling her certainty, not to mention her composure, slipping away under his scrutiny, Rachel said faintly, halfheartedly, "Uh-huh..."

Riley jutted a thumb over his shoulder. "In case you hadn't noticed, the temperature is dropping in here pretty quick. This isn't exactly a fun place to be at the moment."

She gazed beyond his shoulder, at the dead door lying in the middle of Sabrina's living room, and some of her indignation returned. "Oh, and who's fault is that, huh?" she demanded. "Who's going to pay for that door? That door was a rental, you know."

Riley had the decency to look sheepish. "I'm sorry," he said impatiently. "I wasn't thinking when I kicked it in. I saw you moving around in here when I pulled up, and when you didn't answer that first time I knocked, I thought you might be trying to escape.''

She gaped at him. "Escape? From what?''

"From me.''

"Riley...''

His suspicion was so outrageous, she didn't know what to say. So she only shook her head in silence.

He sighed heavily, glancing over at the mess of cookie crumbs on the counter. "Obviously, I was mistaken, all right? I'll have someone take care of the door, and I'll pay for it myself.''

"Terrific,'' she muttered. "The manager is gone for the day. He won't be back until after dark.''

Riley trained his gaze back on Rachel. "I'm sorry,'' he said again. "Looks like you're going to have to find somewhere else to stay for the time being. I'll see if I can't find you a place in town.''

"It doesn't matter,'' she said. "I was going to head back to Oklahoma City tonight anyway.''

His expression grew wary again. "Oh, you were, were you?''

"After I talked to you this afternoon,'' she hastened to add. "After I told you the truth about Sabrina and me.''

"Gee, now why don't I believe that?''

"It's true,'' she said. "I swear it is.''

For a moment, he only continued to look at her. Then he tilted his head toward the front door. "Why don't we just bump up your appointment then?'' he asked. "You can come down to the station right now and tell me all about you and your sister, instead of waiting until later this afternoon.''

"I can't,'' she said with a quick shake of her head.

He nodded knowingly, his mouth twisted into a dubious grimace. "I see,'' he said contemptuously.

"Not because I'm trying to get my story straight,'' she objected, reading his mind, which wasn't all that hard, seeing as how his thoughts were pretty much written all over his face.

Boy, she hoped he'd never had to go undercover as a detective. No way could Riley Hunter ever hide what he was feeling or thinking. For some reason, though, she kind of liked that about him. Then she shook the thought off and reminded herself that she was right in the middle of some major character defending.

"It's not that I can't go with you now because I'm trying to concoct another lie for you," she said.

He still obviously didn't believe her. "Then why can't you?"

"Because I'm waiting for some phone calls."

"Is one of those calls supposed to be from your sister?"

"No. Right now, I'm waiting to hear from some mutual friends of ours who are supposed to be checking with other mutual friends. Honest, Riley," she added softly. "I'm not lying to you. Not now. And I'll tell you everything I know, I promise. Just let me wait to hear from a few people first."

He inhaled deeply and continued to study her face, as if it might have changed now that she was someone else. So Rachel studied him back, wishing they had met on different terms, wondering if there was any chance at all of salvaging...

What? she wondered. How could they salvage something, when they'd had nothing to begin with?

Finding his silence unnerving, she asked, "How did you find out that I wasn't Sabrina?"

For a moment, she didn't think he was going to answer her. He only stood with his hands on his hips in that incredibly sexy way of his—although, now that she thought about it, pretty much everything he did was sexy—and stare at her. At her eyes, at her hair, at her mouth. Just when she thought she'd go crazy from his inspection, and right before she glanced away, he finally responded.

Very softly, he said, "You're not seven months pregnant."

Rachel swallowed hard. Something in the way he said that went way beyond a casual observation. It was as if the realization of her nonimpending state of motherhood held a wealth of significance that she wasn't sure she should ponder.

"No," she replied, every bit as softly. "I'm not. But how did you find out that Sabrina is that far along?"

He smiled, but the action wasn't exactly happy. "The *deus ex fax machine* down at the station told me," he said.

Rachel narrowed her eyes at that. "Excuse me? The what down at the station told you?"

His smile softened some. "Just a little joke. Never mind. Guess you'd've had to major in English to get that one."

She narrowed her eyes at him some more. "I thought your degree was in justice administration."

He nodded. "It is. But I minored in English."

Oh, now *that* was an interesting revelation she never would have suspected in a million billion years. "You, uh, you minored in English?" she echoed. Anything to get them onto another subject, Rachel thought.

He nodded. "Yep, I did. But don't try to change the subject."

Rats.

"When the APB about your sister first came over the fax machine on Friday," he continued with his explanation, "the last page was interrupted midsentence. It said Sabrina Jensen was pregnant, but it didn't tell us how far along. Today we got the rest of the fax, the part that identified Sabrina as a woman who was *seven months* pregnant."

Before Rachel realized what he was going to do, Riley reached out a hand and splayed his fingers across her belly, over the loose, cinnamon-colored corduroy shirt that hung down to midthigh over her battered blue jeans. Although the gesture was gentle, it was in no way ginger. Even through the barrier of her clothing, she could feel that the manner in which he touched her wasn't the way one might cradle a womb that was protecting a baby. No, it was more like the way a man might caress a woman into whose womb he wanted to put a baby to protect.

"Clearly, you're not seven months pregnant," he said softly, his gaze skittering from her flat abdomen back up to her face. His fingers closed more gently, more intimately over her, his thumb tracing a slow circle around her navel that sent her blood racing through her veins.

She swallowed hard, covering his hand with hers, linking his fingers with her own to keep him from driving her even further over the edge. "No, I'm not seven months pregnant."

She wasn't sure, but she thought one corner of his mouth lifted in something that, under other circumstances, might have been a smile. "In fact," he continued, his voice still soft, still smooth, still seductive, "you're not pregnant at all, are you?"

Rachel hesitated for scarcely a moment, then slowly shook her head. "No."

His gaze never left hers as his palm flattened more insistently over her belly, scooting downward a fraction of an inch. "So that means there aren't three men out there vying for paternity of your unborn child, are there?"

She swallowed hard. "No."

"There aren't three men who've slept with you in the past few months."

"No."

"Is there even one man who's...who's made love to you recently? Who's important to you?"

Rachel's gaze collided with Riley's, and she felt pinned in place. Oh, fine. She chose *now* to start being honest with him, when he was asking her things like that. How was she supposed to answer his last question honestly without creating more trouble for herself?

Finally, she decided that a half truth was better than no truth, right? Really, she wouldn't be lying. Just...omitting a little something, that's all. Okay, so what she would be omitting was the full truth. That was beside the point. The point was that there was no reason for him to know how desperately important he *had* become to her. Because there was no way anything could ever come of it. As quickly as he had become important to her, he would fade from her heart. So, why start something that was doomed from the outset?

"No," she said softly. "There's no one who's made love to me recently. Not for a long—" She cut herself off before revealing how very long it had been since she'd made love to a man. It had been years. And lots of them.

But Riley wasn't going to let her off the hook that easily. He noticed as well as she did that she'd neglected to answer his full question. "Or who's important to you?" he prodded her.

Rachel swallowed hard, but didn't answer.

"Rachel?" he asked again.

But there was no way she was going to make a mistake like that. It was bad enough that she'd just *hinted* at how important Riley had become to her over the last few days. No way was she going to tell him outright that she'd pretty much fallen head over heels in love with him.

She gave his hand a gentle squeeze, then reluctantly removed it from its resting place on her belly. The moment the contact was broken, a shiver of cold winter wind swept through the trailer, and she shuddered, in spite of the heat that Riley's touch had ignited in her. Still, she clung to that heat, knowing it would have to get her through a lot more winters than this one. Even if she fell out of love with him the moment she arrived back in Oklahoma City, she was fairly certain that memories of Riley would be warming her for the rest of her life.

Thankfully, he didn't press the line of questioning about who was or was not important in her life. Instead, he rested his hands on his hips again and continued to stare her down.

"Now, then, Miss Jensen," he began again, his voice a little rougher, a little more ragged, than she'd heard it.

"Rachel," she corrected him.

"Rachel," he repeated. Somehow, she got the impression that the name didn't roll as easily off his tongue as Sabrina's had, and that bothered her. A lot. "Why don't you tell me what the hell you're doing living here in your sister's rented trailer? Because I do know that much about the situation. When I spoke to the manager here on Friday, he definitely said Miss *Sabrina* Jensen paid the rent on this place through the end of the year. So, what is *Rachel* Jensen doing here now?"

She nibbled her lip for a minute before answering. In spite of her conviction to tell the truth, she honestly wasn't sure what she should say. So, for now, all she surrendered was, "Like I said— mostly, I'm waiting for the phone to ring."

"Well, Rachel Jensen, you're gonna have a little bit longer wait than you thought," Riley told her. "Because right now, you're coming down to the station with me."

"But—"

"No buts. Either come along peacefully, or I'll run you in the hard way. Whichever way you want to do it, you're coming with me. Now."

"But my phone calls—"

His expression hardened, all of the warmth that had been there a moment ago chilling over like ice. "They'll call back. Now come along nicely. If you're a very good girl," he added in a cool voice, "and if you tell me all the things I want to hear, then maybe, just maybe, I'll be a nice boy. Maybe, just maybe, I *won't* make you spend the night behind bars."

Eight

By the time they arrived back at the police station, Riley still didn't know whether he wanted to kiss Rachel Jensen or shoot her.

On one hand, he was angrier than he'd ever been in his life that she'd lied to him and deceived him the way she had, making him feel both frustrated and foolish. On the other hand, he was just so damned happy to hear that she hadn't been sleeping around with three men. Or even one. She wasn't pregnant and alone. She wasn't a woman in trouble. She wasn't a complete flake whose mental capacity—never mind her morals—were, to say the least, iffy.

Nope, she was just a woman looking out for her twin sister, however...oddly...she'd decided to go about it. And that, Riley supposed, wasn't really a crime at all. Hell, how many times had he done something in his life that he shouldn't have to protect someone he loved? Too many times to count. Still, that didn't change the fact that she had lied to him from the beginning. That she might very well be lying to him still. Best not to get too optimistic where Rachel Jensen was concerned. Not yet, anyway.

Funny, how it had taken him no time at all to adjust to her new name. In a way, it was kind of nice that she wasn't Sabrina, because now the turn of events had a fresh feel, as if they really were starting all over again from scratch. Naturally that didn't mean he had any intention of forgetting about the events of the past weekend. Nor could he ignore the deception that Rachel had played out since her arrival in Wallace Canyon. What Riley *could* do, he told himself, was keep an open mind.

He only wished he could keep that open mind on the matters at hand, and *not* on how cute Rachel looked in those red mittens and that big ol' red hat with its knit cuff riding just above her eyes. Not to mention those snug blue jeans, slashed at both knees, where he could see a pair of white longjohns with yellow flowers on them peeking out from underneath.

Down boy, he instructed a part of his anatomy that refused to heel. He and Rachel had a long way to go before they could start getting deeper into things. Like each other's pants.

As usual, Rosario had abandoned her post without turning off the radio, so the lobby of the station house was empty when they entered, save the sound of Hank Williams—senior, not junior— warbling about being done wrong by yet another love. Virgil had taken the rest of the day off to drive his mother into Felt to do some Christmas shopping before his date with Eloise that evening, so Riley and Rachel pretty much had the place to themselves.

Swell, he thought. For some reason, he felt as if he'd just brought a girl home to meet his folks only to find that they'd been called away overnight, and now he and his date could neck on the couch without fear of interruption. If he and Rachel made it through the interrogation without giving each other a hickey, he supposed they could call it a successful undertaking.

"My office?" he asked halfheartedly, sweeping his hand in that direction.

Without a word, Rachel preceded him, and he found great joy in following behind, watching her, well...her behind. Even with a jacket covering her, the twitch of her hips was just too tempting for Riley to ignore. Rachel Jensen sure did have some way of walking. A walk like that could start fights and stop traffic. Wasn't a man alive could resist something like that.

He growled under his breath at the way his reason—not to mention his self-restraint—seemed to have fled right out the window. He was going to have to sit his libido down tonight over a couple beers and have a real serious chat with it.

"Now then," he said as he circled his desk and sat down behind it, "where shall we begin?"

Rachel, he noted, unsnapped her coat, but didn't remove it. She did, however, jerk off her mittens and cap before dropping into the chair opposite him. But she said nothing to answer his question.

"Fine," he conceded. "We'll just do this the old-fashioned way. Miss Jensen," he began again, this time adopting his formal, I'm the sheriff around these parts and don't you forget it voice, "what were you doing in your sister's trailer without your sister being in residence?"

This time she didn't hesitate before responding. "Sabrina called me at my job in Oklahoma City last week and asked me to come to Wallace Canyon. But by the time I got here, she'd packed up and left."

"So, what made you stay?"

"She called the trailer while I was there. Some of the things she said on the phone made me want to hang around. I thought maybe I could learn something here that would tell me a little more about what was going on."

"She didn't tell you on the phone?"

"No. I asked her to, but she wouldn't."

He thought about that for a moment. "Well, when was the last time you saw your sister in person?"

She inhaled deeply, expelling the breath in a long, low sigh. "Oh, gosh...last summer, I guess," she said. "I'm not sure of the exact date."

Riley did some quick math. "So she might have been pregnant when you saw her. Did you know that? Did she?"

Rachel shook her head. "I don't know if she knew yet or not. She certainly didn't tell me or Daddy about it. I didn't learn about her condition until after she disappeared last fall. She broke down during one of her calls and told me."

"Your parents are still living?"

This time, Rachel nodded. "Not together, but they're both alive, yes."

"They're divorced," he stated, assuming the obvious.

She nodded again. "Since before Sabrina and I started school."

"Has Sabrina contacted your father since she took off?"

"No. When she told me she was pregnant, she made me promise not to tell Daddy. She wasn't sure how to break the news to him. She was afraid he'd be disappointed in her. He still doesn't know."

"And will he be disappointed in her when he finds out?"

"Oh, gosh, no," Rachel was quick to reply. "Daddy could never be disappointed by anything Sabrina did."

Something in her voice made Riley think that maybe Rachel hadn't been so lucky herself in that department, that maybe she'd disappointed their father on more than one occasion. And as much as he wanted to pursue that line of questioning, he stuck to the matter at hand.

"Is there any chance Sabrina may have tried to contact your mother?"

Rachel emitted a derisive sound, and her mouth twisted into a wry smile. "No."

"None?" he asked further, doubtful.

"We haven't heard from Blanche since a few years after she left us," Rachel said coolly. "Not since we were very little girls."

Curiouser and curiouser, Riley thought. Man, he was learning all kinds of things about Rachel Jensen that he wished he'd known before. "So, you don't even know where your mother is now?"

"No. And I don't care, either," she added hastily. But instead of the bitterness the sentiment suggested, her voice was colored by hurt and sadness.

Riley was silent for a moment as he took all this in. Then, changing tack to get to the meat of the matter, he asked flat out, "Do you think one of the Wentworths is the father of Sabrina's baby? Could that be why they're looking for her?"

Rachel, too, took a moment to think about that before she responded. "She's never told me who the father is exactly, but when you told me the Wentworths had put out an APB on her, a lot of stuff she'd said started coming together, and I started to think that, yeah, maybe one of them is.''

Riley nodded. ''That's the impression I've sort of developed myself. But what makes *you* think so?''

She hesitated only a moment before saying, ''When I spoke to Sabrina on the phone Friday, she said her baby's father's family was, and I quote, 'a very prominent Oklahoma family with a lot of money, a lot of power and a lot of influence.' Unquote.''

Riley shrugged. ''There's a lot of rich folks in the state,'' he said for the sake of playing devil's advocate.

''Yeah, but they haven't taken out an APB on Sabrina, have they?''

''No,'' he agreed. ''They haven't.''

Rachel began to chew her lip, as if lost in great thought. As if there was something else she wanted to add, but she wasn't quite sure how to go about it.

''What is it?'' Riley asked. ''Tell me.''

She glanced down at her lap and began to pick idly at a loose thread on her jeans. ''Sabrina said something else about the father's family that you should probably know about.''

''What's that?''

''She said that they...'' Rachel stopped picking at the loose thread and returned her gaze to Riley's face. ''Sabrina is convinced that the Wentworths want to take the baby away from her.''

''*What?*'' Riley had leaned back in his chair, but now he brought the legs forward with a resounding *crack*. ''They want to do what?''

''Sabrina said the father's family wants to take the baby away from her,'' Rachel repeated. ''That's why she ran away. Why she's hiding out.''

''That's crazy,'' Riley countered. ''They can't do that. It's illegal.''

She shrugged. ''People like the Wentworths have a lot of friends in high places. They have ways to get what they want that normal people like you and me would never be able to use. You know what I mean?''

Unfortunately, he knew exactly what she meant. Hadn't Miss

Caroline Merilee Dewhurst's family gotten exactly what they wanted, simply because they had the money and power to get it? They sure enough had rid themselves of Riley, had kept his Cherokee, working-class hands off their pure, lily-white daughter. And not only had they stolen back the woman he loved, they'd made some calls to friends of theirs in the law enforcement field and very nearly cost Riley his job. If nothing else, it had taught him that there were in fact people out there who misused their position in society just because they could.

He nodded. "All right, I'll grant you that folks like that often have means to fall back on that folks like you and me don't. But that still doesn't mean they can take your sister's baby away from her. Or that they even want to."

"Well, Sabrina must think they can and do, because she's run off. And she said some guy was following her, too, a guy she's afraid works for the Wentworths."

"We haven't decided for sure that the Wentworths are the baby's father's family," Riley argued cautiously. There was no sense perpetuating a story that might not be true.

"Well, who else could it be?" Rachel asked him. "Why else would a family like the Wentworths be looking for my sister? She's a waitress, for criminy's sake. And she lives in Tulsa, so she had ample opportunity to have met up with one of the Wentworth boys."

Okay, Riley relented to himself. So there was a good chance that Sabrina had somehow become involved with Michael, or even with Jack before his death. That still didn't explain why they were so fired up to find her, just because she was expecting a baby who might be a potential—

"Heir," he said aloud.

"Air?" Rachel repeated, standing. Quickly, she crossed to the window behind his desk and began to wrestle with the latch. "What's wrong, Riley? Are you okay? You feeling dizzy?"

It took a moment for him to understand what she was doing, and when it finally dawned on him, he chuckled. "No, not *air*," he said. "*Heir*. As in, *Heir to a fortune.* Which is what your sister's baby is going to be. Especially if Jack Wentworth is the father. He's the oldest of the two boys. And he's dead."

Rachel stopped fighting with the window latch as she absorbed Riley's assertion. When he spun himself around in his chair to gauge her reaction, it was just in time to see her sit down on the window ledge, mouth agape, and stare blindly out into his office.

"If Jack is the father of Sabrina's baby," he continued softly, "then your little niece or nephew is entitled to a whole lot of money, Rachel. And a heritage that goes back a long way in this state."

She shook her head slowly, still staring out into space. "I didn't even think about that," she said. "It never even occurred to me that Sabrina's baby—" She smiled, meeting his gaze now. "That my niece or nephew," she corrected herself happily, "would be in a position like that. Do you think that's why the Wentworths want to find Sabrina? Because they want to make sure the baby is *cared for,* and takes his or her rightful place in the family, and not because they want to take it away from her?"

He shrugged, honestly uncertain. "I don't know much about the Wentworths other than what I read in the papers. Although they've been in and out of trouble from time to time, it's always been fairly minor stuff. They don't seem like a bad family. Just too rich for their own good sometimes. I can't see them wanting to find Sabrina and the baby just so they could separate the two of them."

Rachel nodded, but said nothing, as if she, too, were trying to get a handle on this whole thing.

"But being of good Oklahoma stock," Riley continued, "I can definitely see them wanting to do the right thing by the child. I can see them wanting to make sure the baby knows its heritage. Especially if Jack is the father, because if he is, that kid will never know him."

Now Rachel covered her mouth with her hand, her eyes glittering with tears that immediately spilled down her cheeks. "Oh, Riley," she said quietly. "That's so sad. That Sabrina might have this baby all alone, and raise it all by herself because the father is dead. That a whole half of its life will be missing that way. Poor Sabrina. Poor baby."

Oh, no, Riley thought. Not that. Not...tears. Aw, shoot.

If he couldn't resist a woman who was in trouble, he sure as hell couldn't resist one who was crying. In one fluid gesture, he rose from his chair and curled an arm around Rachel's shoulders, leaning back to settle himself against the window ledge to pull her close. Then he wrapped his other arm around her front to link his hands together on her far shoulder, enclosing her in a loose hug.

That was all he did. A totally harmless, totally comforting gesture, just to let her get a good cry out, if that was what she wanted to do. His libido, which was raging and panting just below the surface, was just gonna have to deal with that for now.

Because having a good cry was exactly what Rachel wanted to do. Evidently, she'd been holding in a lot of stuff for a long time now, because with one relentless heave, she threw her whole self into it, clinging to Riley as if she wouldn't be able to stand without him. And Riley just stood there and let her do it, because...because...

Aw, hell.

Because he was half in love with her, that's why. He wasn't sure just how that had happened, or when, but somehow, he knew that the tight tension twisting him in knots was the result of more than simple lust. Simple lust he could have handled, and had on many occasions. Simple lust was the easiest thing in the world.

But this thing for Rachel went way beyond that. In addition to wanting to get physical with her, Riley wanted to get emotional, too. Normally, he'd feel awkward and anxious with a crying woman, in spite of his weakness for them, and would be glancing at his watch to see how much longer she was going to be at it. But with Rachel, he didn't care how long it went on. Because even if Rachel wasn't feeling so hot herself right now, he was kind of enjoying the warm, squishy feelings wandering around inside himself.

He *liked* holding her while she cried her eyes out, he realized. He *liked* it that he could be here for her when she needed someone. He *liked* it that she felt comfortable enough with him that she could reveal the extent of her worry for her sister. He *liked* all that.

He liked it a lot.

So, he retrieved a handkerchief from his pocket and pressed it into her palm, encouraging her to go on as long as she needed to. And while she cried, he rubbed a hand chastely over her upper arm, tucked her head into the hollow of his throat, and murmured comforting words that he wasn't even sure she heard. And when she finally began to quiet down, when she pulled away with a little sniffle and pressed his hanky to her nose, he smiled with as much reassurance as he could.

"It's gonna be okay," he told her, certain somehow that that was true.

She nodded, but he didn't know if she believed him or not. Didn't matter, though. Because Riley was confident that this thing was going to set itself to rights. How exactly that was going to happen, well... He was still a little uncertain about that. One thing was for sure, though. They had to contact the Wentworths. ASAP. He just hoped Rachel wouldn't try to hinder him on that.

"I mean it, Rachel," he said. "Everything's gonna work out. I promise you it will."

She sniffled again, dashing her fingers under her eyes to wipe away the remnants of her tears. "How can you be so sure?" she asked in a shaky voice. "Sabrina is still missing, and nobody knows where she is. Even if the Wentworths aren't trying to take her baby away from her, how do we know the guy following her doesn't mean to do her some harm? And what if something happens to the baby? She's out there by herself and doesn't know anyone. What happens when the baby's time comes? Who'll be with her? Who?"

Riley inhaled a deep breath and released it slowly. "Don't borrow trouble you don't need," he said. "Let's take this one step at a time. There's still a good two months before it's time for Sabrina's baby to come. That gives us two months to find her."

Rachel swallowed, meeting his gaze solemnly. But she said nothing, only waited for him to reassure her some more.

"The first thing we need to do," he said, "is call the Wentworths."

She started to shake her head, then, her gaze never leaving his, she slowly began to nod. "Okay," she agreed softly. "I guess there's nothing else to do. Sabrina won't be coming back here, and you're obviously not the guy who was after her."

It took a moment for that to register. When it did, Riley could scarcely believe what it meant. "You thought *I* might be the guy your sister said was after her?"

Nervously, Rachel scrunched up her shoulders and let them drop. "Well, how was I supposed to know who you were?"

"You knew I was the sheriff of Wallace Canyon," he reminded her.

"Oh, and like you couldn't have been bought off?" she said, some of her earlier fire and indignation returning, much to Riley's relief—even if she *was* using it to insult him. "Like police corruption has never happened before in the state of Oklahoma?"

"Rachel..." he began.

But she cut him off with a wave of her hand. "Look, just let's forget about it, okay? I'll forget I ever suspected you of being a lowlife stalker of pregnant women if you'll forget I was such a...liar."

He smiled. "You weren't being a liar. You were just protecting your sister. Hell, I woulda done the same thing if it'd been me in your place."

"You would?"

He nodded. "I think a lot of people would."

She smiled, a gesture that lit her face up from the inside out, and Riley felt all the air leave his lungs in a quick *whoosh*. Oh, yeah. He had it bad, all right. And, as the song used to say, that ain't good.

And then he remembered something else that wasn't good. Thanks to his overreaction earlier in the day, when he kicked down the trailer's front door, Rachel didn't have anyplace to go while they tracked down the Wentworths. Worse, if she ended up needing to stay over another night, which was likely, seeing as how they were about to travel down a whole new path with her missing sister, then she didn't have a place to sleep. Wallace Canyon wasn't exactly long on tourist attractions—or any other attractions that Riley could identify—and was even shorter on accommodations. People who stayed here stayed with relatives or friends. Rachel didn't have any relatives here. Or friends, either. Just...

Gee, just Riley.

Maybe he could arrange something with Rosario, he thought, pushing away the idea of extending an invitation for her to stay at his place. Having her sleep under his roof probably wasn't a very good idea, what with her being under the influence of heightened emotional upset about her sister and him being under the influence of heightened emotional...uh...sexual hunger. If he could *find* Rosario, anyway, he amended. No telling where she'd wandered off to. Probably doing some more Christmas shopping.

Still, even as the idea formed in his muddled, feverish, over-sexed brain, Riley knew he wasn't going to put up an all-out search to find the receptionist-secretary-dispatcher today. Or ever. So maybe Rachel could just stay at... Oh, gosh, Riley didn't know... Maybe...his place?

Now, why hadn't he thought of that before?

"Rachel," he said, pulling one arm back to settle his hand on his hip. He continued to drape his other arm across her shoulders, however, reluctant to release her completely. She sniffled one final time, wiped her nose and turned red, swollen eyes to Riley. God, she was gorgeous. Even all pink and puffy from crying.

"Yes?" she asked.

"I don't think you should go back to Oklahoma City tonight."

She arched her eyebrows in a silent query.

"It's getting late," he told her, "and that's got to be what...a five-hour trip?"

She nodded. "Depending on traffic. Maybe longer."

"You don't exactly seem to be in the best shape for a long drive right now. You're kinda distracted and upset and all, I mean."

"Yes," she agreed with another sniffle. "That's true."

"And it's supposed to snow tonight," he added. "Not a lot, but still..."

"Oh."

"And once we get ahold of the Wentworths, they're probably gonna wanna talk to you. Maybe even in person. They might even wanna fly out here today, if they can get a flight."

"I guess you have a point."

"So, you might want to reconsider going home just yet."

"Okay."

Well, hell, that was easy, Riley thought.

Rachel turned her face up to his again, her eyes warm and wistful, in spite of their wateriness, as she looked at him. "Since I can't stay at Sabrina's trailer, where's the closest hotel?" she asked.

Okay, so maybe it wasn't as easy as Riley had thought it would be. "Uh...actually..."

"Yes?"

"There, um, there is no hotel in Wallace Canyon."

Her expression clouded with confusion. "What do you mean, there's no hotel here? If you want me to spend the night, then where am I supposed to stay?"

Instead of answering, Riley glanced nervously away.

"Oooh..." Rachel said softly. "You want me to spend the night with you."

"I'll sleep on the couch," he rushed to assure her. "No funny business, I promise. I just..." He sighed. "With everything that's going on with you... I just don't want you to have to be alone, Rachel, that's all." He decided not to add that he didn't want to be alone, either. No sense asking for trouble.

Much to his surprise, she nodded in agreement to his suggestion. "Thanks, Riley," she told him. "I appreciate it. I'd rather not be alone, as a matter of fact. But I'll take the couch. There's no reason for you to be uncomfortable in your own home."

He didn't bother to point out that his cramped apartment upstairs was anything *but* comfortable, regardless of the circumstances. Instead, he only shook his head adamantly and said, "Absolutely not. You take the bed. I'll take the couch. That's all there is to it."

She smiled a little shyly. "Thanks."

He straightened and fished his keys out of his pants pocket, then extended them to Rachel. "I'll call the Freemont Springs PD right now and tell them what I can about the situation. They can contact the Wentworths, and then we'll go from there. How would that be?"

Rachel nodded as she closed her fingers over his keys.

"In the meantime, why don't you get your things out of the truck and make yourself at home at my place?" He jutted his thumb toward the ceiling. "It's right upstairs from where we are now. Just go through the door at the end of the hall."

"Okay."

"You need any help with your stuff?" he offered, even though she'd only brought one small duffel bag with her.

"No, thanks."

For a moment, they only gazed at each other without speaking as an awkward silence descended over the office. Somehow, suddenly, there was a lot more going on than there had been before. Before, there had been a missing woman on the run who needed finding, because she might be in trouble. Now, in addition to that, there was a rampant flow of energy crackling between Riley and Rachel that needed tending to. Immediately.

"I, uh..." Riley began, finally breaking off the silence. "I'll just make that call then."

Rachel squeezed his keys tightly in her hand and took a step backward, toward the door. "And I'll just get settled upstairs."

"Fine," he said.

"Fine," she concurred.

Somehow, though, Riley suspected that it was going to be some time before things between him and Rachel were even close to fine. Worse than that, though, they had a whole night ahead of them to try to straighten things out.

Nine

All in all, Riley's apartment was pretty much what Rachel would have expected of a single man living alone in a place like Wallace Canyon—boring, nondescript and small. And empty. Well, very nearly so, anyway.

A card table and two chairs passed for his kitchen/dining room suite, which was just as well, since the apartment claimed neither a dining room, nor much of a kitchen—unless you wanted to be generous and call the little closet with a stove and pint-size refrigerator a kitchen. The living area—to call it a living *room* would have been an act of charity—boasted nothing but a couch and end table, one lamp, a lumpy chair, and a bookshelf crammed with westerns. And the bedroom—which Rachel only noted briefly, honest—housed nothing but a full-size bed and a single nightstand that played host to a battered lamp and more novels.

Interestingly, there was a laptop computer tucked away on the nightstand's lower shelf, and Rachel wondered what use a man like Riley would have for such a thing. Probably used it for internet dating, she thought uncharitably before she could stop herself. A man like him, stuck out here in the middle of nowhere, sorely lacking for female companionship…

Best not to think about it, she told herself, turning her back on the bedroom entry. No sense making herself crazy over Riley's uh…social needs. After all, she had more than enough to keep her busy going crazy over her own, uh…social needs.

Still, his domain sure was a sparse little apartment. He hadn't even bothered to decorate for Christmas. Not so much as a holly sprig was in sight. For someone like Rachel, who had always embraced the holidays and celebrated them for all they were worth—they were, after all, some of the few times she was guaranteed to see her family—witnessing Riley's total lack of Christmas spirit didn't set well.

He could have at least sprung for a tree, she thought. Certainly there was enough room for that. As long as it was a really, really little tree.

Glancing down at her watch, she noted that it wasn't even two o'clock yet. She'd passed by his office after retrieving her bag from the truck, and Riley had told her that the Freemont Springs PD would be contacting him once they notified the Wentworths. He'd also cautioned that such a call back could take some time, because, according to the Freemont Springs authorities, the Wentworths were rarely at home this time of day.

He'd encouraged her to take a nap or read a book in the meantime, to do something that would help her rest. Rachel supposed that for most people, that was probably sound advice. But there was no way she could sit idle while she was overwrought with concern for Sabrina. An energetic person by nature, taking a load off didn't come easily to her, even under the best of circumstances. Right now, the last thing she wanted to do was sit still.

On her first trip into town Friday, she'd noticed a five-and-dime a block away from the police station. She hadn't brought much cash with her to Wallace Canyon, but Rachel never left home without her American Express. Of course, a place like Wallace Canyon might not take American Express. So it was a good thing she'd been sure to bring her Visa, too.

With a satisfied nod, she donned her coat, hat and mittens, grabbed her purse, and headed for the door. She could be back

in less than an hour, she told herself. And maybe, by then, Rile·
would have some good news.

Riley didn't have any news at all when Rachel returned forty·
five minutes later, clutching two big shopping bags full of holida·
cheer. As she passed by his office on the way back to his apart·
ment, she stuck her head in the door long enough to inquire abou·
the status of his phone call to Freemont Springs. But he just shoo·
his head and mumbled something about no news being goo·
news, but he'd let her know the minute anything developed.

Then he asked her what she had in the bags.

Rachel smiled. "Just a few things I thought I might need," sh·
told him. "Nothing major."

He nodded and waved her off, and she headed toward the doo·
at the end of the hall.

Back up in his apartment, she hummed as she went to work·
first fishing a little plastic, predecorated Christmas tree from on·
of the bags. When she plugged it in, she was delighted by th·
effect, and moved the end table over to the window to place th·
tree atop it. A few long strands of gold-and-silver garland fol·
lowed, which she hung over and down both windows, framin·
the tree. More garland went over the bedroom and bathroo·
doors, and a not-quite-dead-yet poinsettia—the last the store ha·
claimed—became the card table centerpiece. Four votives of red·
and-green speckled glass added a festive touch, especially onc·
she lit the candles within.

Little by little, Rachel turned Riley's spartan, utilitarian apar·
ment into a Christmas wonderland suitable for the season. Wit·
each added decoration, her heart lightened a little, her mood im·
proved, and her worries for Sabrina began to ease.

The Wentworths, she was feeling more confident now, almo·
certainly bore no ill will toward Sabrina. Rachel suspected tha·
like any family, they just wanted to watch over one of their ow·
If Sabrina's baby had been fathered by Jack Wentworth, then, ·
course, the Wentworths would want the opportunity to be part ·
the little nipper's life. Now if Sabrina would just contact som·
body so they could let her know that, then maybe she'd be hom·

for the holidays, and it wouldn't be such a blue Christmas without her.

By the time suppertime rolled around, Rachel was standing on a chair, finishing up with the last of the decorations. She was wrestling a thumbtack through a sprig of mistletoe in an effort to fasten it to the kitchen entryway, when the front door opened, and Riley passed through it.

For one brief, bizarre moment, she waited for him to announce, "Hi, honey! I'm home!" and make his way over to plant a big ol' sloppy kiss on her mouth. Then the moment was gone, and Rachel was spared having to ask him if pot roast was okay for supper, and telling him that she was worried about the Beaver.

"Hi," she said instead. "Soup and sandwiches okay for supper?"

He halted midstride when he saw the transformation that had taken place in his apartment. "What the...?" His voice trailed off, but a smile curled his lips as he took in her handiwork detail by detail.

Only then did it occur to Rachel that she probably should have asked his permission before decorating his place for the holidays. For all she knew, maybe he didn't even celebrate Christmas. And once she was gone from Wallace Canyon, he'd be left to clean up the aftermath by himself.

"I hope you don't mind the decorations," she said belatedly.

He shook his head. "Of course I don't mind. The place looks great. You've been really busy."

Relief wound through her like a swallow of hot chicken soup on a cold winter's day. "I had to do something to stay busy, or I would have gone nuts with the waiting." She shrugged, still clinging to the mistletoe. "I know Christmas is still a week away, but no sense waiting 'til the last minute."

His gaze met hers. "Actually, I hadn't planned to decorate at all."

She wasn't really surprised by the comment, but nonetheless asked, "Why not?"

"Didn't seem to be any point," he told her.

"Why not?" she repeated.

He smiled a little uncomfortably. "Well, why bother if you're not going to be entertaining or having family over?"

She gaped at him. "Why bother?" she said, feeling like a parrot learning to mimic its master's voice. "Because...well, because it's Christmas, that's why."

"Yeah, well, no offense, Rachel, but not everybody celebrates it."

"Oh," she said in a small voice. "I'm sorry. I didn't realize your religious affiliations were—"

"It's not a religious thing with me," he said in as matter-of-fact a voice as she'd ever heard. "It's just... I don't know. I've just never gotten into Christmas, that's all. When I was a kid, my family was too poor for Santa to bring us anything, and we could never afford a tree or decorations. Christmas just wound up being a break from school and a day off for my mom. As an adult... Well, like I said. I've just never gotten into it. It's no big deal, Rachel, honest."

Something chilly and unwelcome landed in the pit of her stomach at his casual observation that his family had been too poor for a holiday and that it was no big deal. The Jensens had been anything but wealthy, and because her father was a trucker, the three of them had spent more than one Christmas on the road. But they'd still always celebrated in small ways the simple fact that they were together.

Her father would duct-tape a little plastic tree to the dashboard of his truck. And he'd tune the radio to a station that was playing Christmas music, so they could all sing along. And even when they wound up having Christmas dinner at a diner or truck stop somewhere, they'd still infect everyone present with the holiday spirit, singing carols and telling stories and having fun.

Too poor to celebrate Christmas? But... Christmas was a state of mind, Rachel thought. Sure, the physical trappings of red and green were nice, and it was always fun to find a gift under the tree. But even without all that...

Christmas was being with loved ones, and sharing and taking care of each other, and helping out people who couldn't help themselves. Christmas was who you were with and how you treated each other, not how good your house looked. It was letting people know how important they were to you. It was giving of yourself, whatever you could afford to give. And suddenly, being with Riley at Christmastime felt like exactly the place where Rachel should be.

"Merry Christmas, Riley," she said softly, still standing on the chair in her stocking feet, afraid to let go of the mistletoe in case it fell.

His expression softened at her greeting, and he moved across the room in a half-dozen easy strides. "I gotta admit," he said when he drew near enough to touch her—not that he did touch her, much to her disappointment, but he was close enough to. "It sure is nice to have someone like you to come home to. In fact, this place has never felt like a home, until now." He smiled. "And that's all your fault, Rachel. What am I going to do with you?"

Something in her belly fizzed merrily at his announcement, bubbling up inside her fast and fierce, bringing with it a little giggle of delight. In response to the sound, Riley's smile broadened, until it was one of those toe-curling, heart-stopping, fire-starting smiles that made her want to leap right into his arms.

"What's so funny?" he asked.

She shook her head. "Nothing. It's just nice to have you home. Any news on Sabrina or the Wentworths?"

He shook his head as he gazed up at her. "Nothing yet. I gave the Freemont PD my home number, though. They're supposed to call me here soon as they have anything. That mistletoe you got there?" he added without missing a beat, pointing with clearly feigned disinterest at the sprig of greenery in her hand.

She nodded, suddenly feeling anxious over the purchase. She'd always bought mistletoe to decorate her own apartment, without ever giving it a second thought—mistletoe was just a part of Christmas. But now, with Riley on the scene, the simple decoration suddenly took on a wealth of significance that it hadn't had at her place. Before, a sprig of mistletoe hadn't resulted in anything more than a quick smooch on the cheek from her father. Now, however...

Uh-oh.

"What can I say?" she asked with a forced casualness that

sounded anything but casual. "I was just feeling kinda whimsical, I guess. But I can't quite get it to stay," she added. "You've got some seriously strong drywall here. I'm afraid if I let go, it's going to fall out again."

"Let me help you."

Before Rachel could tell him no, Riley was tugging off his boots, one by one, and climbing up on the chair with her. If she'd thought her position was precarious before, she was wrong. Because the little chair that had shuddered under her weight suddenly shrank to the size of an electron, and groaned under the combined weight of two people. Worse, with the added burden of Riley, it shifted its center of gravity from the left legs to the right, something that sent Rachel's body crashing into his just as he was lifting his hands to help her with the mistletoe.

For a moment, they froze their positions, until the little chair steadied itself. And then Rachel realized how close their bodies had become, from their entwined fingers overhead to their overlapping toes below. For one scant moment, they stood face-to-face that way, each searching the other's features for some indication of how to proceed. Ultimately, Riley was the one who made the decision for both of them.

With a sly little smile, he threw a silent glance up at the mistletoe before returning his attention to Rachel. Then, very softly, he said, "Merry Christmas, Rachel." And he leaned forward to cover her mouth with his.

It was a tentative kiss, a gentle brush of his lips over hers, as if he weren't *quite* willing to send the chair toppling over by ravishing her the way she found herself wishing he would. Rachel continued to cling to the mistletoe and thumbtack she was holding overhead, something that Riley seemed intent on using to his advantage. Because with her arms lifted that way, he dropped his own, circling her waist quite easily with both arms, splaying open his hands at the small of her back.

And then he did risk intensifying the kiss, pressing his lips more insistently against hers, tracing the outline of her mouth with the tip of his tongue before dipping inside for a soft taste of her.

"Oh," Rachel murmured in response to his delicate invasion. "Oh, Riley..."

But still she held on to the mistletoe, mostly because she was heedless of anything but the feel of Riley surrounding her. From head to foot, he touched her, his breath mingling with hers, his heartbeat pounding in time with her own, the heat in him joining the heat in her, multiplying and growing until a ball of fire zipped through her entire system. And still he kissed her, tasted her, explored her, pressing her closer and closer and closer, until she almost felt as if the two of them really were melting into one.

At last, Rachel released the mistletoe, unable to tolerate not touching him. To her vague surprise, it dangled quite nicely from the entryway above her. Which was convenient, because she still had some serious plans for that little spray of green.

She curled both arms around Riley's neck and twined her fingers in his silky hair, cupping the back of his head and rising on tiptoe to take control of the kiss. When she did, the chair shifted again, tipping both bodies dangerously close to a fall. So, clearly with no small effort, Riley ended the kiss and stepped down from the chair, lifting his arms for Rachel to join him. She smiled as she bent to place her hands on his shoulders, expecting him to lower her to the floor, so they could pick up where they'd left off.

But Riley didn't lower her to the floor. Instead, he scooped her into his arms, hooking one under her knees, the other around her shoulders. For a moment, Rachel just gaped at him in surprise. Then she laughed, a light breath of sound that roused an equally happy response from him.

As quickly as the light, teasing mood had erupted, however, it evaporated, to be replaced by an atmosphere of desire, of longing, of need. As one, their heads dipped toward each other, and as one, their lips joined in a kiss.

This time, there was no tentativeness, no caution, no easy-does-it. Riley slanted his mouth over Rachel's with all the insistence of a man gone too long without sustenance, and Rachel responded as a woman who was equally hungry. Vaguely, she noticed that their bodies began to move away from the chair, but she really didn't care where they were going. All she knew was that she wanted—needed—to be with Riley. Wherever he was, that was where she belonged, and nothing else in the world was of any consequence at all.

Not too surprisingly, he carried her to his bedroom, laying her back on the bed before following her down. Rachel wrapped her arms around him and pulled him close, digging her heels into the mattress to drag both their bodies more fully atop it. Riley nestled himself between her legs, and she opened willingly to him, arching her body slightly to his in welcome.

The weight of him atop her was a delicious sensation, one that sent a thrill of heat and anticipation coursing through her. He touched her everywhere she wanted and needed to be touched, dragging his fingers through her hair, over her face, down her arms and back up again, along her rib cage to her hips. Then he retraced the pattern with an easy, delectable efficiency that left her yearning for more.

So Rachel, too, went exploring, skimming her hands over the satin of his hair, across his broad shoulders and back, down to his taut hips and buttocks, to the backs of his thighs. Riley groaned in response to each of her gentle caresses, intensifying their kiss until she feared he would consume her whole. She urged her hands back up over his body, curving her fingers into his shoulders to pull him nearer, mindless of the fact that they were already as close as two people could be.

Somehow, Rachel wasn't sure exactly when, Riley wedged a hand between their bodies and began to unbutton her shirt. Something—some meaningless, malfunctioning mechanism at the very back of her brain—cautioned her to be careful, to slow down, to think about the repercussions of what they were doing. But what they were doing felt so good, so natural, so...so *right,* that Rachel couldn't see any point to question it. So she ignored the warning, tamped it down, until it finally sputtered and died.

Riley unfastened the last of her shirt buttons as she reached for the first of his. In a less than graceful dance of mingling limbs, he managed to spread her shirt open wide before she'd barely started on his. Beneath hers, Rachel wore an undershirt of the most functional, most unattractive, thermal knit, white with yellow flowers, just like she'd worn when she was a child. She groaned inwardly that she hadn't had the foresight to be born the kind of woman who would go for something skimpy, lacy and black. Because surely a man like Riley Hunter would be looking for that kind of underwear in a mate.

Riley, however, didn't seem to be at all put off by her choice of underthings, Rachel noted. In fact, he didn't seem to notice them at all, because he was too busy working her shirt down over her arms. She helped him as much as she could, lifting her body from the bed so that he could tug the garment off of her and toss it to the floor. But she never stopped working at his buttons while she did. Not until she'd jerked his shirttail free of his pants and unlooped the last one and spread the garment open wide.

And then, Riley helped himself out of his shirt, too, hurling it to the floor alongside Rachel's. For a long moment, he only knelt there between her legs, gazing down at her as she lay on his bed. His breathing was rough and ragged, a perfect match to her own uneasy, uneven respiration. And his eyes...

Oh, my.

Rachel sucked in a quick breath at the absolute need, the raw hunger, she saw burning there. For a moment, she was helpless to do anything but lie there and gaze back at him, taking in the slim build with the elegant musculature, the strong, finely carved features of his beautiful face. His biceps strained at the sleeves of his white T-shirt, its V-neck descending over a smooth chest of umber satin. Slowly, he tugged his T-shirt from his pants and jerked it over his head, letting it, too, fall to the floor. His torso was corded with ridges of muscle, his nipples were flat and coppery, his arms strong and sure.

Rachel swallowed at the clear evidence of his strength, of his power. And she marveled at the scope of her reaction to him. The heat, the sight, the scent of him nearly overcame her. And then he smiled, a smile that was full of planning, of predation, of intent.

"You know, that's the problem with winter," he muttered as he leaned forward over her. He reached for her undershirt and began to tug it free from her blue jeans. "Too daggone many clothes."

Rachel chuckled, a low, sensuous sound she couldn't believe had erupted from her. Why, she sounded like a woman who knew what she was doing, who had a wealth of experience at this kind of thing. She tried not to panic at the memory that she'd been with only one man, only a handful of times, seven years ago. Instead, she focused on her response to Riley. And she forced herself not to think about the fact that history was doubtless about to repeat itself.

One time, she promised herself. Just one time, with Riley. There was no way she could resist him, no way she could turn back now. He'd be her Christmas present to herself, she thought with an inward smile. And this one time with him would sustain her through all the long, winter nights that were ahead in her life. It was all right, she told herself. Because she loved him. And even if that love was destined to last only a short time, it was enough for her to justify what was happening.

Foolish woman, she called herself. But, oh, what memories she'd have to keep her warm...

And then she put even that thought out of her mind, because Riley was urging her up from the bed, pulling at the hem of her undershirt, skimming it up her body toward her head. Without a second thought, Rachel lifted her arms, and with one fluid gesture, he swept it over her. Instinctively, she folded her arms over her small breasts, strangely embarrassed, suddenly reluctant to bare herself to him. Riley had probably had all kinds of lovers in his life, had doubtless seen women far more beautiful, and far better endowed than she.

Yes, he was more than enough to satisfy her, she thought. But how could she have thought she would ever be enough for him?

"Don't," he told her, reaching for her arms to gently pull them away. "I want to see you."

Even as she allowed him to reveal herself, she said with a nervous chuckle, "There's not much to see."

He smiled as he absorbed the sight of her, then returned his attention to her face. "Oh, now, I wouldn't say that."

And before she could stop him—not that she necessarily wanted to stop him—Riley reached out and covered her breasts with his hands, palming both with loving affection. His hands were warm, tender, commanding. And Rachel's heart hammered hard in her chest with every move they made.

"Oh," she said, her eyes fluttering closed. "Oh, Riley."

"See?" he murmured, his voice low and rough. "A perfect fit."

Her eyes still shut tight, she reveled in the sensation of his hands on her, thumbing her nipples, gently squeezing her flesh, rolling her breasts in his palms. Then she felt him move one hand away. She was about to object to his abandonment when his mouth took its place, and he circled her nipple with the tip of his tongue.

She uttered a low, soft sound of surrender, a sound he must have taken as encouragement. Because he sucked her more fully into his mouth, laving her with the flat of his tongue. His hands crept behind her back, opened over her shoulder blades, and he pushed her closer, lapping at her, tasting her again and again. Rachel was barely aware of curling her fingers into his hair and pushing his head closer, until he shifted his attentions to her other breast, and started all over again.

For a long time, he pleasured her so, until she wasn't sure she could tolerate any more. Then, vaguely, she felt him move away, felt his warm mouth skimming over the rest of her torso, felt his tongue dip into her navel as he began to lower the zipper of her jeans. She tried to lift herself up on bent elbows, but Riley opened one hand over her heart and gently urged her back down to the bed. Then he curled both hands simultaneously into the waistband of her jeans and long underwear and panties, pulling gently on all until they passed over her hips, her thighs, her knees, her calves. Her socks came last, and then she lay on his bed clad in nothing but a heated flush that covered her entire body, and the warmth of her love for him.

For a long moment, Riley only gazed upon her in silence. Then, quickly, he moved away from the bed long enough to undress himself the rest of the way. Rachel watched with what she hoped was masked interest as he shucked his pants and briefs and socks. But when he straightened with his legs spread firm and intent, when he stood tall and proud—and naked—staring back at her, when he raked his hands through his hair in an action that was totally lacking in self-consciousness, when he threw her one of those knowing, predatory smiles...

Rachel's mouth and throat went dry as she watched him, as

she enjoyed the ripple of every muscle his body possessed. Inevitably her gaze settled on that part of him that was so very different from herself, that area of his anatomy that would join her body to his. And all she could do was shake her head in wonder and think, *Oh, boy...what have I gotten myself into?*

Riley seemed to understand completely what she was thinking. "Don't worry," he said softly. "I have a feeling we were made for each other. It'll be okay, you'll see."

Then he rejoined Rachel on the bed, once again settling himself between her legs. The feel of his naked body pressing against that most intimate part of her ignited a blaze inside her, a wildfire that swept through her entire system before exploding in her belly. Instinctively, she bucked her hips toward his, in response to the heat, the power, the need.

Riley reacted immediately to her thrust, pushing himself down more insistently against her, pinning her beneath him. "Before we go any further," he said softly, his smile tender, "I want you to know that I'll take care of you, Rachel."

At first, she didn't understand what he meant, thought he was telling her he wanted to be a bigger part of her life than she was sure he ever could be. So she only shook her head in silent denial of the possibility, as much as she wished it could be so.

He must have detected the confusion in her response, because he smiled at her—a smile that was oddly melancholy, she noted—then chuckled softly. "What I mean is that I want to *take care of you*," he repeated, shifting the emphasis of his statement. "I want to use a condom. I hope that's okay with you."

Rachel couldn't have felt more foolish. Of course that was what he meant, she thought. He wanted to take care of her, not *take care of her*. How could she have been so naive?

"Of course it's okay," she said.

He reached for the nightstand drawer and withdrew what looked to Rachel like an Alka-Seltzer packet, something that just went to show how sexually sophisticated *she* was. With little fanfare, Riley extracted and rolled on the condom, and before Rachel could comment, he covered her mouth with his again. This time when he kissed her, it was long and soulful, a kiss of intention, of avowal, of promise. It was a kiss that took Rachel's breath away.

And as she lay there breathless beneath him, his hand crept between their bodies, scooting lower and lower, until he furrowed two fingers into the delicate folds between her legs. She gasped at the contact, looping her legs over his, and he took advantage of both reactions to deepen his exploration, thrusting his tongue into her mouth, penetrating her with one long finger.

Rachel moved her hips against his hand in time with his motions, panting and moaning until she thought she could tolerate no more. And just when she thought Riley's caresses would surely drive her mad, he lifted himself up on bent elbows above her.

"Open your eyes, Rachel," he said.

Only then did she realize she had closed them, and she snapped them open at his command. The face hovering over hers was curtained by silky ebony hair, his dark eyes nearly black with his arousal. And those eyes never once wavered from hers as he nudged her open more fully, only glittered bright with need as he began to push himself slowly into her waiting warmth.

"Oh, you're so tight," he muttered, the words clipped and barely controlled. "Oh, Rachel... Oh, that's so good, honey. So good..."

It was good, she thought. More than good. It was... He pushed himself in farther and she gasped at the full feeling that stretched her with every inch of his arousal. Oh, it was phenomenal.

"Oh, Rachel," he repeated. "I knew we'd be a perfect fit. I knew you'd be..." He swallowed hard. "Bend your knees for me sweetheart. Yes, like that. More. I want to go deeper inside you. You're so... You feel so... Oh..."

Little by little, Riley urged himself deeper into her, and Rachel lifted her hips from the bed to better accommodate him. Slowly, he filled her, took possession of her, became a part of her. She gripped his taut biceps as he shifted his weight, rising higher above her. And still he entered her, deeper and deeper, until she was certain their bodies had completely melded together and become one.

When he was buried inside her as much as he could be, Riley pushed himself up on his hands and began to pull out again.

Rachel wrapped her legs around his waist as he rose to his knees, and, gripping her hips with sure fingers, he quickly pushed himself deep inside her again. Over and over he withdrew and advanced, the friction of his body moving inside hers sparking a response in Rachel unlike anything she'd ever felt before. As he tipped his head backward, her eyes fluttered closed, and blindly, she focused on the sensations rocking her.

Faster and farther they climbed, racing toward an apex she could never have anticipated. She circled his forearms with rigid fingers and squeezed hard as he hurried his pace, lifted her body to greet each heavy stroke of his own. And then, with one final, furious thrust, Riley shoved himself deep inside her, stirring a spiral of electricity that shuddered through her, sparking heat throughout her entire system.

Rachel cried out at the exquisite perfection of their culmination, and Riley unleashed a roar of pleasure that echoed her own. For one long moment, their bodies remained arched, motionless, to receive the full pleasure of their union. Then he slumped forward against her, gathering her close, burrowing his damp head against her neck.

When he murmured something unintelligible against her shoulder, Rachel couldn't help but smile. Whatever it was he'd said, it couldn't be any more confusing than the thoughts and realizations spinning through her head. She refused to pay heed to any of them, though, and instead wound her arms around Riley to pull him closer.

Later, she told herself, knowing she was only asking for trouble. Later, she would give way to all the second thoughts she knew would inevitably assail her. Right now, she wanted only to think about Riley. About the way he made her feel. About the way she felt for him. About making love with him again, because that one time she'd been so sure would last her a lifetime had only roused a hunger in her that was nowhere close to being satisfied.

Later, she repeated to herself, forcing every other thought from her head for the time being. Later...

Ten

Riley wasn't sure right away what woke him. When his eyes fluttered open, he was aware of only one thing: a total and profound feeling of happiness that suffused his entire soul, a sensation unlike anything he had ever felt before. For a moment, he couldn't understand what had caused such an odd reaction. Then, gradually, it dawned on him that he wasn't alone in his bed, that there was a warm, wonderful body pressing intimately against his own. And that was when it hit him, what had brought him such unmitigated joy.

Rachel.

Oh, yeah. Now he remembered. Boy, did he remember.

With a smile, he started to turn toward her, to snuggle closer and draw her more fully against him. Then he heard the sound of his phone ringing in the other room. As hastily and carefully as he could, he extracted himself from Rachel's side, doing his best not to wake her. Without even bothering to dress, and heedless of the chill that had settled over his apartment, he raced for the phone. He counted four rings in addition to however many else had come before them by the time he snatched the phone off the receiver. Consequently, the quick greeting he barked was probably less than cheerful.

"Sheriff Hunter?" a woman's voice came from the other end of the line, concerned and uncertain.

"That's me," he replied. "Can I help you?"

"Detective Marilyn Robinson," she identified herself. "Freemont Springs, Oklahoma PD. I was just about to hang up."

Riley scrubbed a hand brusquely over his face in an effort to chase away the leftover muzziness from too little sleep and too much loving. Then, in spite of himself, he smiled salaciously. As far as he was concerned, there was no such thing as too much loving when it came to Rachel Jensen.

"Sorry about that," he muttered into the phone, pushing away, for now, his illicit thoughts about their recent union. "I was, uh... I fell asleep and just now heard the phone."

"But it's not even nine o'clock."

"It, uh, it's been a long day," he said. "What have you got for me?"

Detective Robinson sighed. "Well, nothing on the missing woman yet, but the Wentworths are delighted that you've found her twin sister. They'd like to fly her out here as soon as possible."

Riley straightened. Fly Rachel out to Freemont Springs? Way over on the other side of the state? Now? When the two of them were just getting to know each other?

"Why?" he asked.

Detective Robinson's hesitation told Riley she thought he should already know the answer to that question. "Because she's their only link to Sabrina Jensen right now, that's why," she said. "They'd like to meet Rachel, to ask her about her sister, seeing as how Sabrina is pregnant with the child of their late son, Jack. They're naturally curious about the baby's mother."

So it was true, Riley thought. Jack Wentworth was the father of Sabrina's baby.

He was about to say something else when he felt a tentative hand cup his bare shoulder. He turned to find Rachel standing behind him, wrapped in the bedspread, her hair all sleep-rumpled, her eyes all dewy and bright, her mouth swollen and reddened from the vigorous loving the two of them had shared. And just like that, Riley was hard as a rock and very anxious to end the conversation with Detective Robinson.

"Who is it?" Rachel asked.

Instead of answering, Riley spoke into the phone. "Detective Robinson," he said reluctantly, "I have Rachel Jensen here with me right now."

"Oh, do you?"

Riley didn't like the speculation that was unmistakable in the other woman's voice. Then again, he supposed he'd set himself up for it. First claiming to have been sleeping, now revealing that Rachel was with him. Still, that was none of Detective Robinson's business, was it?

For now, he chose to ignore the woman's tone of voice and asked shortly, "Would you like to speak to her?"

"Put her on."

He handed the phone to Rachel. "It's a detective from the Freemont Springs PD," he said. "Detective Robinson. The Wentworths would like to meet with you."

"With me?" she said, clearly puzzled as she reached for the phone.

Riley nodded, but said nothing, only tuned his ear to eavesdrop on Rachel's side of the conversation that ensued.

"Yes, I'm Sabrina Jensen's twin sister," she said in response to the detective's query from the other end of the line. "No, I'm afraid I have no idea where she is." She listened a moment longer, then said, "Last Friday, on the phone..." She shook her head at something the detective said, then added, "All I know is that she was at a bus station, waiting for a bus to take her somewhere. I *can* tell you that she *wasn't* going to Lincoln, Nebraska, but that's about it..."

For a good ten minutes, Detective Robinson grilled Rachel on her relationship with her sister, and on what Sabrina's last known whereabouts or next known intentions might be. But Rachel could offer her no more information than she'd already given Riley. He listened with half an ear as he returned to his bedroom and fished a pair of blue jeans and a gray sweatshirt out of the chest of drawers in his closet, then hastily dressed. When he returned to the other room, Rachel was nodding at something Detective Robinson was telling her, and gripping the bedspread around herself as if it were the only thing that linked her to reality.

"But why do the Wentworths want to meet with me?" he heard her ask. She listened intently for a moment, before replying. "All right. No, that's fine. I'll be happy to. But instead of flying I'll have to drive. I have my car here. Tell them thank you, anyway. I can be there by tomorrow evening."

After a brief exchange about Rachel's travel plans, she handed the receiver back to Riley. "She wants to talk to you again."

He took the phone from her, then watched as she, too, returned to the bedroom, presumably to dress. "Yes?" he said as he pressed the receiver to his ear, concerned not just about the slump to Rachel's shoulders as she made her way across the room, but also about the cold swirl of discomfort circling in his own belly.

"Sheriff Hunter, do you think there's any chance that Sabrina Jensen will be returning to Wallace Canyon?" Detective Robinson asked.

"I really doubt it. She doesn't have any ties to the community. Sounds like it was just a fluke that she ended up here in the first place. I don't look for her to be coming back."

"Well, if you do have contact with her, you'll let us know, right?"

Riley's lips twisted into a wry smile. No, he'd sorta planned on keeping that kind of information to himself. Duh. "Yes ma'am," he said to the detective. "Y'all'll be the first to know."

"In the meantime, please be aware of the fact that the Wentworths, and the Freemont Springs PD, appreciate everything you've done with regard to Miss Jensen. Your role in this case has not gone unnoticed."

"Just doing my job, detective."

With nothing more to be said, Detective Robinson signed off with a benign wish for Riley to enjoy the holidays, then terminated the connection at her end. So he, too, settled the receiver back in its cradle, and wondered what he was supposed to do now.

Rachel would be leaving in the morning. That much, if nothing else, was certain. And Riley wouldn't be going with her. That unfortunately, was certain, too. Even if Wallace Canyon was a sleepy little community, he couldn't just up and abandon his post any time he wanted to. Yeah, there might not be a whole hell of a lot of responsibility in this particular position, but Riley wasn't a man to shirk an obligation, no matter how small.

Maybe he could get away for a few days after the New Year, he thought. Drive over to Oklahoma City, see how Rachel was doing. He hadn't taken any time off since starting his job as sheriff. Surely Virgil and Rosario could manage for one weekend without him. Especially if he waited until the new moon, so the notorious howling Barker family would be at their ebb.

"Rachel?" he called out when she still didn't return from the other room. "You okay in there?"

"Fine," she returned, her voice sounding very small and distant. "I'm just packing up the few things I unpacked this afternoon."

He took a few tentative steps toward the bedroom, not liking the sound of her response. "Why don't you wait and do that tomorrow, sweetheart?" After all, he could think of lots of better ways to be spending what looked to be like their last night together for a while.

She hesitated for a moment before answering, "I'd just as soon go ahead and get on the road. It's going to be a long drive to Freemont Springs, and since I'll be by myself, I'll want to take a lot of breaks. Hey, no time like the present, right?"

Wrong, Riley thought, hastening his stride. *Wrong, wrong, wrong.*

"What do you mean, you'd just as soon go ahead and get on the road?" he demanded as he rounded the bedroom door.

He saw Rachel dressed in a different pair of blue jeans than she'd had on before, an oatmeal-colored sweater riding low on her hips. Her back was to him, and she was stuffing a pair of socks into her duffel bag. But she said nothing in reply to his question, nothing to counter his assertion that she'd be leaving him right away.

So Riley asked her again. "You're not suggesting that you're gonna start off for a drive across the state tonight, are you?"

She kept her back to him as she began to tug the zipper on her bag closed. "Why not?" she asked. "I just had a good nap. I could make it two or three hours before I have to stop. Um, can I have my car keys back? Please?"

Riley's back went up fast at the way she just blew off what had been a life-altering experience for him. If she thought for one minute that he'd believe she hadn't been as affected by their lovemaking as he had, then she had another think coming.

"You just had a hell of a lot more than a good nap," he said. "And don't you forget it."

That, at least, made her spin around to look at him. Granted, the expression on her face wasn't one that was all dreamy and needful and loving, the way he'd hoped she'd be feeling about now. But at least she was looking at him again.

She licked her lips nervously, tucking a wayward strand of hair behind one ear. Then, in a very tight voice, she said, "Riley, what happened here tonight—"

"Don't," he interrupted her, lifting a hand to cut her off. "Don't you dare stand there and tell me that what happened between the two of us a little while ago was just one of those crazy things."

Her cheeks flamed pink, and her lips narrowed into a thin line. "No," she agreed softly, her voice touched with just the kind of longing he was feeling himself. "It wasn't that."

"Or that it was a mistake, either."

"No, it wasn't a mistake, either. But it still shouldn't have happened."

"Why not?"

She sighed heavily, a sound of resolution that he didn't like one bit. "Because it won't happen again, that's why. It can't happen again."

He forced a smile. "Sure it can. Right here, right now. I'll give you a send-off before you leave for Freemont Springs that you won't likely soon forget."

She nodded. "And that's what it would be, Riley. A send-off. I won't be coming back here again."

He'd suspected as much, but hearing her say it flat out that way...

"I understand," he said. "And I can't say as I blame you.

Wallace Canyon's not exactly a hotbed of opportunity. But, Rachel, that doesn't mean—''

This time, she was the one to raise a hand to interrupt him. "It's not that," she said.

"Then what?"

She studied him for a long time before answering, with a scrutiny that left Riley feeling as if he'd been turned inside out and upside down, only to be deemed insufficient.

"I do care for you, Riley," she said softly, earnestly. "Truly I do."

"Why do I think I hear a 'but' coming?"

Ignoring his question, she continued just as he had suspected she would. "But I'm the kind of woman who falls in and out of love *a lot*. I think that right here, right now, I can honestly say that I love you."

He opened his mouth to pounce on that, but she cut him off again before he could complete what he was going to say.

"But by this time next week," she said, her voice growing a little shaky, "you'll be out of my mind."

"I'll be out of your mind," he echoed incredulously, thinking she had it backward. Hell, she was the one who was out of her mind.

She nodded, but said nothing.

"After what happened here tonight, do you honestly think you can put me out of your mind that easily?"

"It's not that I *want* to put you out of my mind," she objected, "it's just that you *will* be."

"I don't believe you."

"It always happens that way with me, Riley. I've never been able to stay in love for more than a few weeks at a time. I'm just not made for anything long term."

"You don't honestly believe that."

"Yes, I do. It's the way I am. The way I've always been, ever since I was a teenager."

"Had a whole mess of lovers, have you?"

She shook her head. "No. Just one before you."

"Then how do you know you're as flighty as you say?"

"Because within days of that one lover leaving me, I was halfway gone on someone else. And then, within a few days of meeting him, I met someone else I fell in love with.''

''And how old were you at the time?''

''Seventeen.''

He expelled an incredulous sound. ''Hell, Rachel, I fell in and out of love all the time when *I* was seventeen, too. Everybody does. That's no proof that I can't be in love with you now.''

''You're...you're in love with me?''

''Well, hell, yeah, I'm in love with you. Couldn't you tell? I thought I just went out of my way to show you how much.''

She shook her head. ''You'll get over it. Just like I will.''

''Don't count on it.''

''Trust me, Riley, that's the one thing I *can* count on in life. That I can't fall in love with one man for any length of time. I take after my mother that way. It's genetic.''

''I don't think a fickle heart is genetic,'' he said.

''It is in my family.''

''Rachel—''

''Riley, don't. Just let it go.''

''No.''

''Riley—''

''What we have isn't like what I've had with anyone else. Even after such a short time, I know that. I *know* it, Rachel. And I think if you'll look deep inside yourself, you'll see that you know that, too.''

For a moment, she only gazed at him in silence, as if she were indeed delving into her soul to search for the truth in his allegation. But instead of smiling and throwing herself into his arms upon reaching a revelation, instead of telling him, *Hey, what do you know, you're right,* Rachel only shook her head slowly and reached behind herself for her bag.

''I have to go,'' she said softly. ''Thank you for all your help, Riley. I'll let you know when I hear something from Sabrina. Now then. Give me my car keys. Please.''

Reluctantly, he retrieved her keys from a dresser drawer and handed them to her. But before he could say another word, she moved forward and pushed right past him. He was just opening his mouth to tell her to stop when he heard the front door click shut behind her. And he promised himself then that, come hell or high water, there was no way he'd let Rachel Jensen disappear the way her sister had.

All in all, the Wentworths seemed like very nice people, Rachel thought when she met them late the following afternoon. She was exhausted from her drive across the state, sore—both physically and emotionally—from the extensive lovemaking she and Riley had enjoyed. And she was still heartsick over her sister's continued absence—among other things. So she wasn't in the best of conditions to be meeting folks, even those to whom she would be irrevocably bound through her sister's baby for some time to come.

Still, Detective Robinson had told her how eager the Wentworths were to make her acquaintance, how desperately they wanted some link—however tenuous—to the mother of the late Jack Wentworth's child. Rachel would have felt like the meanest woman on the planet if she hadn't agreed to meet with them. So, as much as she'd wanted to pick up I-35 South as she'd passed it, and head home to Oklahoma City, she'd kept on driving 51 East until she'd found her way to Freemont Springs.

And now she was glad that she had. Although Sabrina's whereabouts were still unknown, the Wentworths seemed a bit less anxious now than they had been upon Rachel's arrival a half hour ago. As she sat in the poshly appointed living room of the stately Wentworth mansion—a room, incidentally, that was roughly twice the size of her studio apartment back in Oklahoma City— she took them in one by one.

Joseph Wentworth was the epitome of Rich Family Patriarch, elegantly attired in a charcoal suit and wine-colored silk necktie, his once dark hair liberally threaded with silver. He was fully at ease in his luxurious home, surrounded as he was by his family and the housekeeper he'd introduced as Evelyn. She obviously doted on the Wentworth children the way a loving aunt would, and was clearly just as deeply grieved over Jack's death as his blood kin.

Josie Wentworth, Joseph's granddaughter and Jack's younger sister, was seated next to her new husband Max Carter—who also happened to be Rachel's cousin, another tie to the family she couldn't overlook—and appeared to be happy and content in her newlywed state. Her dark brown eyes were alive with speculation, her auburn hair stylishly blunt cut, swinging about her shoulders with every animated move she made.

Max, too, looked happier than Rachel had ever seen him, though it had been a while since she'd spent any time with her previously grouchy cousin. She remembered him as always being grim-faced and ill at ease around others, not to mention intensely private. Josie had brought out a side of him that Rachel sure had never seen, a side that suited him nicely. The two of them had made no secret about the baby they were expecting next summer, and were clearly awaiting the arrival with utter joy.

Michael Wentworth, with his dark hair and eyes, was every bit as good-looking as his sister, and he took the word *charming* to new heights. If Jack had been anything like his younger brother, Rachel could see how Sabrina would have been completely swept off her feet. Michael had flirted shamelessly with Rachel from the moment she'd stepped in the door, but with her mind on other matters, the last thing she felt like doing was flirting back. Sure, he was cute and everything, but, hey...

He wasn't Riley.

All in all, Rachel couldn't imagine her sister Sabrina being a part of such a family. As nice as they were, the Wentworths of Freemont Springs were a world away from the truck-driving Jensen nomads. Their obvious riches, their privileged background, their elevated social ties—all of it was so foreign to Rachel. Certainly they were pleasant people, but they were also very intimidating. She hoped that when Sabrina was found, her sister wouldn't feel as out of place among them as Rachel did.

"You'll have to forgive us, Rachel," Joseph Wentworth said, bringing her attention back to the conversation from which she'd wandered with her preoccupation. "I know we've overwhelmed you since your arrival, but you must understand that we've been so very curious about the mother of Jack's baby. How the two of them met, what Sabrina is like. If you find us staring at you with a certain lack of discretion, it's because we know we're seeing a mirror image of the woman Jack loved."

"Jack loved Sabrina?" Rachel asked.

Until that moment, she honestly hadn't considered Jack's feelings for Sabrina. Although she was certain her sister must have loved the baby's father—Sabrina never would have put herself in such a position if she hadn't been completely, overwhelmingly in love—Rachel hadn't really given much thought to his response to Sabrina. She'd supposed that, like other men, courting Sabrina had been little more than a pastime to Jack Wentworth. It was comforting to know that he'd genuinely cared for her as more than a good time.

"Oh, absolutely Jack loved her," Josie piped up. "We're certain he'd even planned to propose to her before he...well..." She sobered quickly, but a squeeze from Max had her smiling again, however sadly.

"He wanted to marry Sabrina?" Although, by now, Rachel had come to believe that the Wentworths would do right by Sabrina's baby, she had still wondered what her sister's role in the scheme of things would be. But if Jack had intended to marry her... "Does Sabrina know that?" she asked.

"We don't think so," Josie said. "But there was a ring among my brother's personal effects, along with a letter and snapshot of Sabrina. It only makes sense that he intended to give that ring to your sister. There'd certainly been no one else in his life lately. Or ever."

Rachel nodded, praying to herself that Sabrina called her again soon, so she could tell her sister all of this. Maybe it would make a difference. If Sabrina knew the Wentworths didn't want to do anything to hurt her or the baby, if she knew Jack had intended to make her a Wentworth, too, then maybe it would be enough to lure her back home. Where she belonged.

"Can you tell us more about her?" Josie said. "Your sister, I mean?"

Rachel smiled. "Well, Sabrina didn't tell me anything much about her relationship with Jack. She wouldn't even tell me his name." Rachel had already told the Wentworths about Sabrina's suspicions where the family was concerned, and although they'd been hurt and surprised, ultimately, they'd understood Sabrina's fears. "And even though I'm a mirror image of my sister," Rachel continued, "don't think for a moment that by meeting me, you're meeting Sabrina. There are a lot of differences between us."

"Such as?" Michael asked, his voice once again carrying a smooth, flirtatious interest that Rachel would have to be a fool to mistake.

And again, she easily ignored it. "Sabrina's much more levelheaded than me. She makes plans and sticks with them until they're complete. If she puts her mind to something, it gets done. Pronto."

"And you're more…impulsive?" Michael asked.

He smiled a smile that might have taken Rachel's breath away under other circumstances. If she hadn't had her mind on something—or rather, some*one*—else.

"I tend to live my life by the seat-of-the-pants school of thought," she said in response to his question. "*Qué será, será,* and all that. Me, I never know where I'll end up. But Sabrina's not going anywhere unless she makes plans first, traces the route on a map, gasses up with a full tank, and packs a healthy snack to tide herself over."

Rachel wished she'd made a few plans before her last trip through the wonderful world of life experience. Then maybe she wouldn't be sitting here thinking about Riley and feeling so heartsick.

"It sounds like Sabrina will be a good mother to her and Jack's baby," Josie said, her voice warm and wistful.

Rachel nodded. "Sabrina will be a great mom. She's loving, responsible, generous to a fault. It's just too bad that the baby won't get to know its father."

A somber silence fell over the group, and Rachel wished she could take back the words, even if the thought she'd voiced was, more than likely, the one on everyone's mind at the moment.

"Well," Joseph spoke up gruffly, "we'll just have to do our best to make sure the baby gets to know the rest of the Wentworths. Especially since he—or she—will be one, too."

"Y'all really do want to make Sabrina and her baby a part of the family, don't you?" Rachel asked. Even though she already knew the answer to the question, she was a little surprised by the family's closeness and generosity.

"Well, of course we do," Josie told her. "They already *are* a part of the family. I just wish Sabrina would turn up so we could let her know that."

"I'm sure she'll call me again soon," Rachel said. "Christmas is almost here. She was supposed to spend it with me and my father in Oklahoma City. Even if she doesn't show up, I know she'll call. She'll have to. If not on Christmas Eve, then surely on Christmas Day."

"I just hope you're right," Joseph said. "That would be the most wonderful Christmas present of all."

Rachel hoped she was right, too. Because the longer they went without hearing from Sabrina, the more worried she became that something bad had happened to her sister. And every day brought them closer to the baby's due date. Sabrina was seven months pregnant. A lot of babies came early. What happened if Sabrina's was one of them? What happened if her baby came while she was out in the middle of nowhere, with no one there to help her?

Don't think that way, she admonished herself. Sabrina was fine, Rachel was sure of it. And she would call soon. She was due to spend Christmas with Rachel and their father, and none of them had missed that holiday together yet. Surely, Sabrina would come home for Christmas. Surely, she would. And then, with the three of them reunited, that would only leave one person missing from Rachel's holiday.

Riley.

Because regardless of her assurances to the contrary—to him and to herself—Rachel had the feeling it was going to be a long, long time before Riley was out of her head, out of her heart. The two of them had made love, after all—sweet, delicious, magical love—and that was bound to make him harder to forget than the others. Still, she was certain she would forget him. Eventually. Someday. Not *too* far in the distant future.

Until then, however... Well, suffice it to say that Rachel wasn't looking forward to Christmas this year with nearly the glow of happiness she normally had about now. As much as she hated to acknowledge the feeling that was fast winding through her, something told Rachel that she and her father were going to be alone on Christmas, waiting for Sabrina to call. And waiting, and waiting, and waiting...

Eleven

Actually, Rachel did receive a call on Christmas Eve. But it wasn't from Sabrina. It was from her father.

"I can't make it this year, sweetheart," he said from what sounded like a very great distance. The connection was bad, full of distortion, and she could barely make out what he was saying. Still, she'd heard the most important part.

"Not coming?" she cried into the receiver. "But you *have* to come! Daddy! We've never missed a Christmas together."

"I'm sorry, Rachel," her father said. "But I'm stuck in a bear of a blizzard up here in South Dakota. Ain't nobody leaving this state for a long time. Your old man included."

Rachel turned her gaze to the big window in her living room that looked out onto a tiny park behind her apartment building. Fat snowflakes were falling fast and furious in Oklahoma City, too, and had been since she'd awoken that morning. Still, it was nothing like the blizzard he described. He should have been almost to Kansas by now—he was supposed to have arrived at her apartment by suppertime. Now it looked as if he'd be having his supper—and his Christmas—elsewhere.

She sputtered into the phone, "But...but—"

"Don't worry about me, sweetheart," her father interrupted her. "I found me a motel, and there's a real party atmosphere here. Lots of people who got stuck on their way home for the holidays. We're gonna make our own holiday here. There's a van full of church ladies whipping up eggnog and cookies in one of the kitchenettes, and we got a whole mess of monks from God knows where with a big ol' truck full of cheeses and fruitcakes. Trust me—I'll be full of the holiday cheer."

Oh, fine, Rachel thought. *He'd* be full of the holiday cheer. Where did that leave *her?*

"But, Daddy—"

"I have to go, sweetheart. There's other people who wanna use the phone. I just wanted to let you know I won't make it by tonight—or tomorrow, or the next day—but that I'm safe and sound here, so don't be worryin' about me. I should be able to get outta here in a few days, though. I could make it to your place by New Year's Eve, okay?"

"But—"

"Give Sabrina a kiss for me, when she gets there."

"But, Daddy, that's just it. Sabrina—"

"And tell her that I love her, okay, Rachel?"

"But—"

"And I love you, too, sweetheart. Y'all have a merry Christmas, and I'll see y'all in less than a week."

"Daddy, wait—"

But it was too late. The buzz of a disconnected line hummed in her ear. Her father hadn't even told her where he was staying. She couldn't even call him back to wish him a merry Christmas.

And now she was going to be alone for the holiday. Because she hadn't heard a word from Sabrina since that last phone call in Wallace Canyon that had thrown Rachel together with Riley Hunter. And deep down, somehow she knew that her sister wouldn't be contacting her again. She'd told Rachel she feared for her safety. If there was one thing twins always did, they watched out for each other. If Sabrina thought it would endanger Rachel to contact her, then she wouldn't do it. Period.

So that left them all back at square one.

Well, not quite square one, Rachel thought. There was that business about her having lost her heart to Riley Hunter that was totally different from where she had been in the beginning. A week had passed since she'd seen him, and there had been absolutely no change in her feelings for him.

Oh, wait, she quickly amended. That wasn't quite right. There *had* been a change in her feelings for him. They'd intensified. A hundredfold. She loved him more now than she'd ever loved anyone. Why, even Michael Wentworth's continuous flirting had done nothing to take her mind off of—

Wait a minute. Michael *had* flirted outrageously with Rachel that day at the Wentworth home, she recalled. And she hadn't felt even one twitter of desire to flirt back. He was unbelievably handsome, phenomenally charming, yet she hadn't for one moment felt inclined to succumb to his obvious interest in her. He was attractive, witty, adorable, sexy, all the things that normally combined to create a man who would be Rachel's downfall. Michael Wentworth was, in short, a real cutie.

Yet he'd left Rachel cold. All she'd been able to think about was Riley.

The doorbell erupted then, shaking her from her revelation. She opened it to find a delivery man on the other side, holding in one hand a box about the size in which one might wrap a basketball. When Rachel took it from him, he extended a clipboard toward her and requested her signature on it.

After completing the gesture, she glanced up and found that the deliveryman in question was tall and blond and gorgeous, with the name *Helmut* embroidered over the pocket of his navy blue uniform jacket. The color highlighted his midnight blue eyes, and his smile was... My goodness, but it was dazzling. He was young and adorable...and he was smiling back at Rachel as if he'd just as soon forget about the rest of the deliveries he still had left to make the day before Christmas.

Hmmm... A small experiment would not be out of place here, Rachel decided.

"Rachel Jensen," he said, reading her signature from the clipboard before throwing her a look that was positively scandalous.

She nodded. "That's me."

"So..." he began again, stringing the word out smoothly. He leaned insouciantly in her doorway and arched one eyebrow in a way that was most becoming. "You, uh...you got anything needs...delivering?" He wiggled his eyebrows in a way that went well beyond suggestive.

Rachel waited for the fizz of delight and anticipation that normally erupted in her belly right about now, whenever a handsome man started making his lascivious intentions known. And then she waited some more. And waited, and waited, and waited...

For nothing.

She realized then, much to her surprise, that a little one-on-one time with Helmut the Dashing Deliveryman was the last thing she wanted to indulge in at the moment. Hey, she had other things on her mind right now. A father caught in a blizzard, a pregnant sister on the run, a gorgeous sheriff stuck out in the wilds of Oklahoma's no-man's-land whom she was heart and soul in love with, so would it be okay if Helmut just shoved off and never darkened her door again?

Aloud, she only said, "No thanks, Helmut. Take a hike." And then, with absolutely no trouble at all, she closed the door in his face.

Wow. She was two for two when it came to having absolutely no interest in a man who was clearly interested in her. That was amazing. Maybe she should spend Christmas Eve barhopping, to see just how many men she could find herself uninterested in.

Then again, why bother? she thought. Because, even though she'd been a little slow on the uptake, she realized now that there was only one man she was going to be interested in for the rest of her life. And maybe, if she hurried, she could be at his place by nightfall.

She was about to glance down at her watch, but her gaze fell on the return address of the package Helmut had just delivered.

It was from a boutique in Oklahoma City, a little shop she'd made no secret was her most favorite retail establishment in the whole, wide world. Curious, she ran her thumb under the tape and tore the box open. Inside, she found a gaily wrapped package and a tiny card.

Even without opening it, she knew the gift was from Sabrina. Though whether her sister had actually been in Oklahoma City recently, or had simply telephoned in an order from miles away, Rachel had no idea. She withdrew the envelope from the card and realized the message was written in a hand other than her sister's. So Sabrina hadn't bought the gift in person. She wasn't in Oklahoma City. She was miles away, and she wasn't coming home for Christmas.

Rachel read the inscription on the card through a blur of tears.

Merry Christmas, Rachel.
I wish I could be there. But I take heart knowing Daddy will be with you, and you won't be alone. I'm not alone, either. I have the baby to keep me company. Both of us are fine. We hope you are, too. I miss you and love you. And Daddy, too. Tell him that, okay?

                                        Love, Sabrina.

With a melancholy sigh, Rachel tucked the card back into its envelope, then made her way to the tree on the other side of the room, and added Sabrina's gift to the meager assortment of presents lying there. One she'd purchased for her father. Another for Sabrina. A handful from some of her ex-regulars at the bar from which she'd been fired.

But none of them held what she really wanted for Christmas. And there was one glaring absence in the gifts she'd bought for loved ones.

It was still early, she thought. The stores were still open. She could run out real quick and pick up something for Riley, then come back and pack a bag and head west. Even with the snow, she could be in Wallace Canyon by nightfall. And then she could spend Christmas in the traditional way, and be with the one she loved.

Be with the one who loved her.

Without further hesitation, Rachel donned her coat and hat and mittens, snatched her purse off the kitchen table and headed out the door.

Where the hell could she be on Christmas Eve? Riley wondered as he pressed Rachel's doorbell for the tenth time. She'd made such a big deal out of her family being together at her place, yet her place was disturbingly empty, and it was almost dark outside. If she was celebrating here with her family, then dammit, she oughta be here. But obviously, she wasn't.

Daggone it.

He'd waited too long to come, he thought. Obviously, Rachel had made other plans. Shoot, all he'd wanted to do was surprise her, show up on her doorstep the day before Christmas, thinking maybe she'd consider it a wonderful present. Even if she *had* made it clear in no uncertain terms the last time they'd seen each other that she wouldn't be seeing him again. He'd just figured she'd been like he was that night at his apartment—scared to death of what was happening between them. And where his way of dealing with fear was to face it head-on, clearly Rachel's way was to turn tail and run as fast as she could.

But, hell, he'd thought by now she'd come running back. If nothing else, he figured he could spend the holidays bringing her around to his way of thinking.

And here he'd gone and deputized Billy Barker and let Virgil take over as sheriff of Wallace Canyon until they found a replacement to fill in for Riley full-time. Because with the presents he had in his sack, he'd been planning on making Oklahoma City his new home. Permanently.

He was about to push the doorbell again, then sighed heavily in defeat. Rachel wasn't home, and it didn't look as though she was going to be home anytime soon. He might as well just look for a hotel for the night. Great. He was going to be continuing what had become his one holiday tradition this time of year—spending Christmas alone. Well whoop-de-do.

Just as he was turning to make his way back toward the front door of Rachel's apartment building, he heard someone—someone really loud and mad—coming in from the outside. He took a few tentative steps down the hall, craning his neck around the stairwell to see if there was any kind of imminent threat coming at him from the other side. He saw a big, down-filled parka, knee-length, hood up, with two snow-encrusted snow boots sticking out of the bottom, and about eight shopping bags and duffel bags jutting out from the ends of what appeared to be arms.

Nanook of the Nativity, was the first thing that came to Riley's mind. Then, gradually, the sounds Nanook was making started to sound kind of familiar....

"Daggone blizzard," the bundle muttered loudly. "Winter Wonderland, my eye." Then, to no one in particular, the owner of the parka began to sing, slightly off-key and very angrily, "Sleigh bells *stink,* are you listenin'? In the lane, snow is...snow is... Well, it's keeping me from the man I love. A horrible sight, I'm ticked off tonight, stranded in a Winter Wonderland."

Riley grinned at the lyrics, focusing on the ones that had sounded angriest of all. The part about her being kept from the man she loved. Funny, he and Rachel must have had the same idea—spending Christmas together, each at the other's place. He'd had a heck of a time driving to Oklahoma City from Wallace Canyon through snow that had just become thicker and heavier the farther he'd driven, and he'd left at daybreak. He could only imagine what kind of weather Rachel must have encountered heading in the opposite direction. Obviously, the snowstorm had grown bad enough that she'd had to turn around.

And as mad as she obviously was about that development, boy, was Riley happy about it.

She stomped up the three stairs that led from the landing to the hallway, never once looking up, never ceasing her grumbling, leaving little piles of snow in her wake. She was about to run right over Riley when she must have sensed his presence and came to an abrupt halt. She glanced up—at least, he thought she was glancing up; it was kind of hard to tell with that big ol' hood wrapped around her face—and expelled a little sound of disbelief. Then she dropped everything she was holding and shoved the hood back from her head.

Oh, yeah. It was Rachel, all right. He'd know those eyes—that smile—anywhere.

"Hey, there," he said. "I was just wondering what you were planning to do for the holidays."

In response to his question, she hurled herself into his arms, wrapping hers around his neck before covering his mouth with her own. Not one to ignore such an invitation, Riley roped his arms around her waist and kissed her back. For a long time, they stood entwined in the hallway, kissing, touching, tasting, renewing feelings they'd never quite got a handle on to begin with. Only at the sound of a door slamming upstairs did Riley finally end the kiss. Very reluctantly, at that. Still, they could always pick up where they left off later.

"So, what are you doing for Christmas?" he asked again.

"Spending it with loved ones," she told him, smiling. "Or, at least, loved one. You."

He arched his eyebrows in surprise. "What about the rest of your family?"

Her eyes clouded over some, but even the reminder of her missing sister didn't completely rob her of her happiness at seeing Riley again. "No word from Sabrina, except for a package that arrived this morning. She sounds like she's safe, though. And Daddy's stranded by a blizzard in South Dakota. He won't be able to make it until next week."

"Gee, too bad," Riley said without a trace of regret. "Guess that just leaves you and me."

"Guess it does."

"Come on," he said softly. "I'll help you carry your stuff in."

Together, they collected Rachel's scattered belongings, but when Riley reached for one shopping bag in particular, she grabbed his sleeve and snatched it out of his hands.

"No peeking," she said. "It's Christmas."

He arched his eyebrows in surprise. "I hope that no-peeking rule only applies to presents, and not other things."

She smiled suggestively as she straightened and fished her keys out of her pocket. "Like what?"

But he only smiled in response, far more suggestively than she.

The moment they were over the threshold, Rachel dropped her burdens on the floor, shut the door and locked it, and flicked the switch that turned on the Christmas tree. The sun had set almost completely, and the apartment was awash in soft, variegated light that flickered off and on at irregular intervals, multiplying as it reflected off all the shiny decorations.

"Wow," Riley said. "This place looks great. You went to a lot of trouble."

"Yeah, well, I only do this for people I love, and don't you forget it."

Riley turned to offer her a knowing look. "I thought you said you'd be over me by now."

She gazed back at him a little sheepishly. "Yeah, well, about that..."

"Yes?"

"I, uh..." She cleared her throat indelicately. "It would appear that I was grossly mistaken about that. I hope you won't hold it against me. But I'm afraid it looks like I am in fact irrevocably in love with you. It looks like I'm going to stay in love with you from now until, oh, gosh...eternity, I guess."

"Gee, what a coincidence," he replied. "That's pretty much exactly how long I'm going to be in love with you."

She shook her head. "Who knew?"

Riley threw up his arms in the ages-old gesture of *Hey, got me.*

"We have a lot to talk about," she said softly.

He nodded. "Yes, we do."

"Do you mind if we do it over supper?" she asked. "I'm starving. I got all the way to Guymon before I had to turn back, but with all the snow and traffic, it took me forever to get here. And I didn't want to stop to eat, because I was afraid of getting stranded."

"Funny. I didn't want to stop to eat, because it meant that much less time to spend with you."

She smiled. "How about a cheese ball?"

Riley smiled. "Only if it comes with something other than wine."

"You're in luck. I just so happen to have about two gallons of eggnog in the fridge. Daddy loves it."

"Gee, so do I."

Riley followed Rachel into the kitchen, not just to help her out, but because he simply did not want to be more than a few inches away from her. He was rewarded with the sight of her shedding her clothing, layer by layer, until she stood before him in nothing but a long-sleeved thermal underwear T-shirt and jeans. How a woman could make something like long johns sexy, Riley would never know. Then again, Rachel Jensen could make a rubber chicken suit look sexy.

Riley, too, discarded his outer clothing until he was down to a denim work shirt and jeans. And he had to admit that there was something about the sight of their boots, sitting side by side atop the heat register, that set something to warming in his midsection. Together, the two of them withdrew the makings of a Christmas feast from the refrigerator—sliced ham, cranberry sauce, bean salad, rolls—then added the traditional touches of fruitcake, eggnog, Sociables, and, of course, the cheese ball. Rachel spread a brightly colored quilt on the living room floor beside the Christmas tree, and together, they enjoyed a Christmas Eve picnic that Riley was just sure was bound to become a family tradition.

When they'd finished their feast and stowed the leftovers, they returned to the living room with coffee, taking their places on the quilt again. By now, they'd distributed an added assortment of gifts under the tree, and Rachel eyed them with undisguised anticipation.

"You know," she said, "I always hated having to wait 'til Christmas morning to open presents. I always wanted to tear through them on Christmas Eve."

Riley smiled. "No one's stopping you now."

She wrinkled her nose indecisively. "Yeah, but there's still something nice about the anticipation. I like opening them Christmas morning, too."

"Then compromise," he told her. "Open one tonight, and the rest tomorrow."

"Funny, that's what Daddy always let us do when we were kids. Open one on Christmas Eve."

Riley shrugged. "Go for it."

Evidently, Rachel already knew which one she wanted to open, because she reached for one of the ones Riley had brought with him. It was a cube-shaped box the size of a teacup, and she lifted it to her ear to shake it lightly.

"It rattles," she said.

"Mmm-hmm," he replied noncommittally, tamping down the thrill of fear that bubbled up inside him. Boy, did he hope she liked what he'd gotten her.

She lowered the box to her lap and withdrew another from under the tree, handing it to Riley. "You have to open one, too," she told him.

"Okay."

Riley, too, shook his present, and it rattled even more than Rachel's. "What is it?" he asked.

"Open it."

Never one for preliminaries, he ripped the paper from the package and found an industrial-size box of Lorna Doone cookies underneath. He smiled. "It's just what I wanted," he said. He nodded toward the gift Rachel still clutched in her hand. "Your turn."

She, too, went right to work, tearing the paper from the box in no time at all. Then she opened it and withdrew another box, this one smaller, and made of black velvet. She glanced quickly up at him, a half smile dancing about her lips.

"Go on, open it," he repeated.

Slowly, cautiously, Rachel folded the top of the box backward, gasping softly when she saw what was inside—a ring, consisting of a small emerald nestled in a crush of sterling silver.

"It reminded me of your eyes," he said. "I was hoping you might wear it as an engagement ring. I know diamonds are more traditional, but they're just way too common. They don't suit you at all.''

When Rachel glanced up again, the eyes that so reminded Riley of emeralds were filled with tears. But she said nothing in response to his assertion that he hoped she'd wear the ring as a symbol of their marital intentions. The fear that had rippled to life inside him suddenly exploded into a full-blown panic. She'd said she loved him, he reminded himself, and would for all eternity. Still...

"Will you marry me?" he asked, surprised at the anxious whisper that replaced his normally robust voice.

The tears in her eyes spilled over at his question, and, very softly, she said, "Oh, Riley..."

She finished her response by hurling herself forward, into his arms, and fastening her mouth to his. Okay, he was pretty sure that qualified as a big ol' yes, and the panic that had begun to burgeon inside him subsided. For a long moment, the two of them only entwined their bodies and kissed each other senseless. Then, finally, Rachel pulled away and pushed the box toward Riley.

"I want you to put it on my finger," she said.

He readily complied, withdrawing the ring from the box with exquisite care before gently sliding it over the ring finger of her left hand. Immediately, Rachel held her hand aloft, admiring the play of Christmas lights in the emerald. Then she dropped her hand to Riley's face, cupping his jaw in her hand.

"I love you," she said softly.

He covered her hand with his and leaned forward. "I love you, too."

"Forever," she added.

"Forever," he agreed.

Rachel, too, leaned forward, meeting him halfway. What ensued was a kiss that might have changed the world, had it been enjoyed by more than two people. As it was, it changed Rachel and Riley's world. And really, that was all that mattered. The warmth of his mouth on hers sent a heat winding through her that was more incandescent than the sun. And all she could think was that she'd just received the most wonderful gift in the world.

And then she ceased to think at all, because he leaned forward some more, pushing her easily backward until she lay beneath him on the quilt. Above his head, the bright lights of the Christmas tree twinkled merrily, and she smiled as she threaded her fingers through his hair. Then he kissed her again, and her eyes fluttered closed, and her other senses took over. He tasted of coffee and smelled of evergreen, and the heat of him seeped through the fabric of his shirt to warm her palms and fingertips. Blindly, she felt for the buttons on his shirt and unfastened them one by eager one. Riley sensed her intentions immediately, because he came to her aid right away.

In no time at all, they had helped each other out of their clothing, and they lay naked, hot and eager beneath the tree. He buried his head in the tender flesh where her throat joined her shoulder, kissing her softly before skimming the tip of his tongue over her skin with much affection. He even nipped her lightly, an action that made her gasp with delight, before laving the wound with his tongue again, bringing forth a groan of satisfaction from deep inside her.

She tangled her fingers in his hair as he moved lower. He skimmed his parted lips over the sensitive flesh of her breast before mouthing her hungrily, enclosing her in a mixture of warm breath and moist possession. Again and again, he suckled her, teasing her, tasting her, taunting her, until she wasn't sure she could stand his assault any longer. She moaned as she splayed her hands open over his bare back, reveling in the strength and satin heat she found there.

"Oh," she murmured. "Oh, Riley..."

Her softly uttered response must have inspired him, because, vaguely, she felt him moving lower still, dragging his open mouth over her torso, across her flat belly, dipping briefly into her navel as he passed. Then, somehow, it registered in her feverish brain that he had moved between her legs and was spreading them wider, draping her knees over his shoulders. Rachel was about to ask him what he thought he was doing, when she received an answer, loud and clear.

"Oh," she cried out as his tongue darted against that most intimate part of her. "Oh, *Riley...*"

He tasted her with outrageous intention, parting her, moving deeper, then retreating to tempt her again. Rachel writhed beneath him, seeking purchase, and found her hands anchored in his hair once again. But instead of pulling his head away, as she told herself any decent woman would do, she found herself feeling deliciously *in*decent, and pushing him closer to her still. She wasn't sure how long they lay there, perhaps minutes, perhaps weeks, but the sensations that rocked her seemed to go on forever.

"Oh, please..." she finally murmured when she was sure she could tolerate no more. "Riley..."

He must have sensed the urgency in her voice, because he slowed his assault and moved leisurely up her body again, briefly sampling her breasts once more as he passed them. Then, without hesitation, he rose up on his knees, gripping her hips fiercely in both hands. Instinctively, Rachel circled his waist with her legs, and before she could say a word, he buried himself deep inside her, as far as the two of them could be joined. Together, they cried out at the intensity of their coming together. Then, for a moment, they stilled.

And then, Riley moved inside her, and Rachel arched herself against him, to pull him deeper. Their gazes held as they generated a rhythm that started off slow and sensual, gradually building to fast and furious. Again and again they bucked against each other, until, with a feral growl, he thrust himself forward one last time, emptying himself inside her.

For a long moment, they remained motionless that way, while the repercussions of the union shook them both to their cores. Then, as one, they slowly relaxed, Riley bending himself protectively over Rachel before stretching out alongside her. He cupped her jaw in his palm and kissed her, long and hard and thorough. Then he moved back only far enough to let him look down into her face.

"You know, you never did tell me for sure if you'd be my wife," he said softly.

And although, at this point, Rachel figured he should be fairly certain what her answer would be, she stroked her fingers gently over his jaw, and told him quietly, "You bet I'll marry you, Sheriff."

For some reason, the word *sheriff* made him frown. Before she could comment, however, he said, "Actually, I'm not a sheriff anymore."

She arched her eyebrows in surprise. "You're not?"

He shook his head. "I, uh...I quit."

She opened her mouth in quiet astonishment. "You did?"

He nodded, then pulled the side of the quilt up over them, to ward off the chill that was fast overtaking their damp bodies. Then he nestled closer to Rachel in their cocoon, bending one elbow to rest his head on his hand as he stroked her cheek with his other.

"I've been sorta working on another project for a while now," he said. "Since I moved to Wallace Canyon. And it looks like the time spent on it has paid off."

Rachel, too, lifted a hand, weaving her fingers lightly through Riley's hair before skimming her fingertips over his cheek, his jaw, his mouth. What could she say? She just couldn't get enough of touching him. "What kind of project?" she asked.

If she hadn't known better, she would swear he blushed at her question. Surely, it was just a trick of the Christmas lights, she told herself.

Still, he sounded a little sheepish as he said, "I, uh, I kinda wrote a book."

She smiled. "You did? That's so cool."

He nodded. "What's cooler is that some publisher up in New York bought it. Just yesterday. Offered me a two-book contract, in fact."

"Riley!" she exclaimed happily. "That's so great! What a wonderful Christmas present. What kind of book?"

"A, uh...a western. I've always loved Louis L'Amour and Zane Grey. It's kinda along those lines."

She linked both arms around his neck and pulled him down for a quick, congratulatory kiss. "I'm so happy for you. No wonder you quit as sheriff."

"The advance for the two books isn't real big, but it's more than what I was making in Wallace Canyon. And now I can live anywhere I want."

"Like maybe Oklahoma City?" she asked hopefully.

"Like *definitely* Oklahoma City," he told her. "Or wherever you want to live."

"No, I like it here," she said. "I was even thinking of enrolling at OSU."

"Studying...?" he asked.

"Business," she told him. "I figure if Sabrina can run her own business, then I can run my own business."

"What kind?"

She shrugged. "Haven't decided yet."

"Whatever you do," Riley said, "you'll be great at it."

The reminder of her sister sobered Rachel then. "I wish she was home," she said. "That's the only thing that would make this Christmas better, having Sabrina...and Daddy...here."

"She's safe, Rachel," Riley told her. "You know she is."

"I'd rather have her here. With her family. But I don't know what to do. How to let her know that the Wentworths don't mean her any harm. That they want to make her and the baby a part of the family."

"You know," Riley said, "I've been thinking about that myself. I know a woman who writes for the Tulsa paper. She and I go way back."

"Oh, really?" Rachel said, unable to quell the ripple of jealousy that wound through her, even knowing how Riley felt about her. "Just how far back do you and she go?"

He smiled, clearly enjoying her reaction. "I'm the godfather of her son."

"Oh."

"Anyway, I thought maybe I could contact her about your sister. See if she could write a story on the search. Maybe if Sabrina read it, found out how everybody wants to help her, then maybe she'd come home. Or they could print a picture of Sabrina, and maybe somebody who's seen her would come forward."

Rachel nodded as she thought about his suggestion. "That's a great idea, Riley,'' she said. "We should call the Wentworths right now and see what they think."

She saw him glance over her head at the clock on the end table. Then he glanced back down at her. "It's kind of late to be doing that right now, sweetheart. It's after midnight."

She smiled. "It's Christmas Day," she said.

He nodded, smiling back.

"Merry Christmas, Riley."

"Merry Christmas, Rachel. And thanks for giving me what I wanted most in the world."

"Lorna Doones?" she asked with a smile.

He shook his head. "You."

She smiled again as she pulled his head down to hers for another kiss. And as her lips met his, she thought about how nice it was that they'd both gotten exactly what they wanted for Christmas.

* * * * *

FOLLOW THAT BABY into Silhouette Yours Truly
in January 1999
when rising star Christie Ridgway
tells the charming story of
THE MILLIONAIRE AND THE PREGNANT PAUPER.
And the following month, look for the concluding title in
the series: THE MERCENARY AND THE NEW MOM
by Merline Lovelace,
Intimate Moments, February 1999.

*Read below for a sneak preview
of the next fabulous*

Follow That Baby title,

THE MILLIONAIRE AND THE
PREGNANT PAUPER

by rising star
Christie Ridgway,

*available in Silhouette Yours Truly
in January 1999...*

The two-hundred-year-old grandfather clock in the foyer wheezed. Michael Wentworth burrowed deeper into the library's leather couch and counted each raspy gong...seven... eight...nine.

Hell. Three more hours until midnight.

New Year's Eve. A playboy's Night of the Year. Who would believe on tonight of all nights, instead of guzzling champagne and nuzzling beautiful women, he was counting clock chimes like Cinderella?

But that wasn't right. Cinderella possessed a healthy fear of midnight. Michael was more eager than a racehorse at final posting call for Baby New Year to show up on the doorstep.

Ding dang ding dong. Michael groaned, not because of the clock this time, but the stuffy, stentorian tones of the front doorbell. "No one's home!" he yelled in the direction of the door.

With the staff off for the evening, he'd counted on being alone all night.

Ding dang ding dong. That damn doorbell again. "We've all gone away!" he yelled again, but got up and marched toward the door anyway. He reached the entryway just as the annoying doorbell started up again.

"Keep your pants on," he grumbled and pulled open the heavy wrought-iron-and-glass door.

A waif stood before him, wearing jeans, a parka and a wide-eyed expression of shock.

"I'm Beth Masterson," the woman said in a breathy voice. Her hands tightened into fists and two white teeth clamped down on her lower lip. A moment passed, then she released a long breath. "I'm sorry to bother you, but I'm going to have a baby."

The bells and chimes had affected his hearing. "Pardon me?" he said. Only the dim beams of the foyer's sconces touched her—he hadn't bothered to turn on the outside lights—and her white-blond hair glowed like moonlight against her dark parka. She shifted, and the ends of her hair swept over the blue nylon. "I'm—" she started again. Her hands recurled into fists and a visible shiver ran through her body.

"For God's sake—" Cupping her upper arms, he pulled her inside, then shut the front door. The slick fabric of her coat felt cold beneath his palms, and he spun the nearby rheostat to add the illumination of the foyer chandelier.

She squinted against the blazing light and winced. Blue eyes. Lips nearly blue with cold, too.

Small, ringless hands crept over the parka toward her middle. "I'm really sorry, sir." She visibly swallowed. "But as I told you a minute ago—I'm going to have a baby!"

A dozen thoughts formed in Michael's mind, even as he ushered her to the closest seat in the foyer.

What was a young and unwed pregnant woman doing on the Wentworth doorstep?

She couldn't be the missing pregnant woman the Wentworth family was hunting for. He'd seen Sabrina Jensen's picture and she looked nothing like this delicate waif.

She couldn't be a woman he'd dated then somehow forgotten. He never went without protection, and even on a hell-raising night he wouldn't forget that moonbeam hair.

So why—

Her fingers closed over his wrist. "I think—" Her voice stopped, and then grew strong like her grip on him, both reinforced by steel. "I need to get to the hospital *now*."

That galvanized him.

Terrified him, too.

Within minutes he bundled her into his truck. With the heat on full blast and the mysterious woman at semirecline on the passenger side, his sheepskin-lined coat thrown over her for extra warmth, Michael finally had a second to think through a few pressing particulars.

"I've got a cell phone," he said, darting a quick glance her way. "What's the number of the baby's daddy? I'll call him for you."

Her mouth tightened and then she tried a little smile. It wobbled a bit before she gave up. "It's 1-800-HE'S-GONE." She made a second valiant attempt at a smile.

It wasn't a big smile, but a smile so real, so genuine, that—

That he couldn't wait to reach the county hospital, which this moment was looming on his right. This lady with her smiles and her arriving baby were nothing to him. Nothing beyond the Good Samaritan responsibility to get her to the delivery room on time....

But somehow he knew that wasn't true, just as surely as he knew his whole life was about to change....

* * * * *

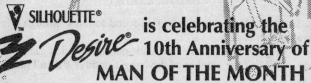

SILHOUETTE® is celebrating the
Desire® 10th Anniversary of
MAN OF THE MONTH

For ten years Silhouette Desire
has been giving readers the ultimate in
sexy, irresistible heroes.

So come celebrate with your absolute favorite authors!

JANUARY 1999
BELOVED by Diana Palmer—
SD #1189 Long, Tall Texans

FEBRUARY 1999
**A KNIGHT IN RUSTY ARMOR
by Dixie Browning—**
SD #1195 The Lawless Heirs

MARCH 1999
**THE BEST HUSBAND IN TEXAS
by Lass Small—**
SD #1201

APRIL 1999
BLAYLOCK'S BRIDE by Cait London—
SD #1207 The Blaylocks

MAY 1999
LOVE ME TRUE by Ann Major—
SD #1213

Available at your favorite retail outlet, only from

Silhouette®

Take 2 bestselling love stories FREE

Plus get a FREE surprise gift!

Special Limited-Time Offer

Mail to Silhouette Reader Service™

3010 Walden Avenue
P.O. Box 1867
Buffalo, N.Y. 14240-1867

YES! Please send me 2 free Silhouette Desire® novels and my free surprise gift. Then send me 6 brand-new novels every month, which I will receive months before they appear in bookstores. Bill me at the low price of $3.12 each plus 25¢ delivery and applicable sales tax, if any.* That's the complete price, and a saving of over 10% off the cover prices—quite a bargain! I understand that accepting the books and gift places me under no obligation ever to buy any books. I can always return a shipment and cancel at any time. Even if I never buy another book from Silhouette, the 2 free books and the surprise gift are mine to keep forever.

225 SEN CH7U

Name		(PLEASE PRINT)	
Address		Apt. No.	
City		State	Zip

This offer is limited to one order per household and not valid to present Silhouette Desire® subscribers. *Terms and prices are subject to change without notice.
Sales tax applicable in N.Y.

UDES-98   ©1990 Harlequin Enterprises Limited

Follow
That Baby

FOLLOW THAT BABY...

*the fabulous cross-line series featuring the
infamously wealthy Wentworth
family...continues with:*

THE MILLIONAIRE AND
THE PREGNANT PAUPER
by **Christie Ridgway**
(Yours Truly, 1/99)

When a very expectant mom-to-be from
Sabrina Jensen's Lamaze class visits the Wentworth
estate with information about the missing heir, her baby
is delivered by the youngest millionaire Wentworth,
who proposes a marriage of convenience....

Available at your favorite retail outlet, only from

Silhouette®

Look us up on-line at: http://www.romance.net

SSEFTB4

For a limited time, Harlequin and Silhouette have an offer you just can't refuse.

In November and December 1998:

BUY ANY TWO HARLEQUIN OR SILHOUETTE BOOKS and
SAVE $10.00
off future purchases

OR BUY ANY THREE HARLEQUIN OR SILHOUETTE BOOKS AND **SAVE $20.00** OFF FUTURE PURCHASES!

(each coupon is good for $1.00 off the purchase of two
Harlequin or Silhouette books)

JUST BUY 2 HARLEQUIN OR SILHOUETTE BOOKS, SEND US YOUR NAME, ADDRESS AND 2 PROOFS OF PURCHASE (CASH REGISTER RECEIPTS) AND HARLEQUIN WILL SEND YOU A COUPON BOOKLET WORTH **$10.00** OFF FUTURE PURCHASES OF HARLEQUIN OR SILHOUETTE BOOKS IN 1999. SEND US 3 PROOFS OF PURCHASE AND WE WILL SEND YOU 2 COUPON BOOKLETS WITH A TOTAL **SAVING OF $20.00**. (ALLOW 4-6 WEEKS DELIVERY) OFFER EXPIRES DECEMBER 31, 1998.

I accept your offer! Please send me a coupon booklet(s), to:

NAME: _____

ADDRESS: _____

CITY: _____ STATE/PROV.: _____ POSTAL/ZIP CODE: _____

Send your name and address, along with your cash register receipts for proofs of purchase, to:

In the U.S.	In Canada
Harlequin Books	Harlequin Books
P.O. Box 9057	P.O. Box 622
Buffalo, NY	Fort Erie, Ontario
14269	L2A 5X3

PHQ4982

SILHOUETTE® Desire®

COMING NEXT MONTH

#1189 BELOVED—Diana Palmer
Long, Tall Texans
Beguiling Tira Beck had secretly saved herself for Simon Hart, January's
10th Anniversary Man of the Month. But this long, tall Texan wouldn't give
beautiful Tira the time of day. And she wasn't about to surrender her *nights*
to the stubborn-but-irresistible bachelor…unless he became her beloved!

#1190 THE HONOR BOUND GROOM—Jennifer Greene
Fortune's Children: The Brides
His prestigious name was the *only* thing formidable businessman
Mac Fortune was offering pregnant, penniless Kelly Sinclair. But once this
dutiful groom agreed to honor sweet Kelly, would he love and cherish her,
too?

#1191 THE BABY CONSULTANT—Anne Marie Winston
Butler County Brides
Father-by-default Jack Ferris desperately needed instruction in baby-
care basics. And Frannie Brooks was every toddler's—and every virile
man's—dream. Now, if Jack could only convince the sexy consultant to
care for his child…and to help him make a few of their own!

#1192 THE COWBOY'S SEDUCTIVE PROPOSAL—Sara Orwig
A simple "yes" to Jared Whitewolf's outrageous proposal and
Faith Kolanko would have her dream: a home *and* a baby. But she wanted a
husband, too, not some heartbreaker in a ten-gallon hat. Could a ready-
made marriage turn this reckless cowboy into a straight-'n'-narrow spouse
and father?

#1193 HART'S BABY—Christy Lockhart
Zach Hart wasn't about to open his ranch to sultry stranger Cassie Morrison
just because he and her baby shared a strong family resemblance. He had to
beware of fortune seekers…and their adorable, chubby-cheeked children!
Then again, what could it hurt if they stayed just *one* night…?

#1194 THE SCANDALOUS HEIRESS—Kathryn Taylor
Was the diner waitress really a long-lost heiress? Clayton Reese had fallen
so deeply for the down-to-earth beauty that he wasn't sure if Mikki Finnley
was born into denim or diamonds. This lovestruck lone wolf had no choice
but to find the truth…and follow his heart wherever it might lead.